TOUCH OF EON

EON WARRIORS
BOOK 2

ANNA HACKETT

Touch of Eon

Published by Anna Hackett

Copyright 2019 by Anna Hackett

Cover by Ana Cruz Arts

Edits by Tanya Saari

ISBN (ebook): 978-1-925539-64-6

ISBN (paperback): 978-1-925539-65-3

WHAT READERS ARE SAYING ABOUT ANNA'S ACTION ROMANCE

Heart of Eon - Romantic Book of the Year (Ruby) winner 2020

Cyborg - PRISM Award Winner 2019

Edge of Eon and Mission: Her Protection - Romantic Book of the Year (Ruby) finalists 2019

Unfathomed and Unmapped - Romantic Book of the Year (Ruby) finalists 2018

Unexplored – Romantic Book of the Year (Ruby) Novella Winner 2017

Return to Dark Earth – One of Library Journal's Best E-Original Books for 2015 and two-time SFR Galaxy Awards winner

At Star's End – One of Library Journal's Best E-Original Romances for 2014

The Phoenix Adventures – SFR Galaxy Award Winner for Most Fun New Series and "Why Isn't This a Movie?" Series

Beneath a Trojan Moon – SFR Galaxy Award Winner and RWAus Ella Award Winner

Hell Squad – SFR Galaxy Award for best Post-Apocalypse for Readers who don't like Post-Apocalypse

"Like Indiana Jones meets Star Wars. A treasure hunt with a steamy romance." – SFF Dragon, review of *Among Galactic Ruins*

"Action, danger, aliens, romance – yup, it's another great book from Anna Hackett!" – Book Gannet Reviews, review of *Hell Squad: Marcus*

Sign up for my VIP mailing list and get your *free box set* containing three action-packed romances.

Visit here to get started: www.annahackett.com

CHAPTER ONE

D amn, this fabric was soft. Lieutenant Lara Traynor ran her hand down the cloak she wore. The material was a silky gray, repelled water, and was super-warm against the incoming chill of night. It also hid her weapons perfectly.

The Eon sure knew how to make high-tech accessories.

She flicked the large hood up over her head, and then turned a corner. She slipped into the small crowd walking through the stone-lined street.

God, she was on an Eon moon. In Eon territory. Her pulse jumped slightly. After joining the Earth Space Corps as a teenager, she'd dreamed of seeing parts of the Eon Empire. Of course, the alien species had made first contact with Earth decades before...and promptly wanted nothing to do with Earth's brand of messy, chaotic disorder. First contact had *not* gone well, and the warriors had banned any Terran from entering Eon space.

And that was a shame, because the Eon had all kinds of high-tech goodness.

Now, Lara had her boots on the tiny moon called Tholla. It orbited one of the Eon homeworlds, Ath. The other three homeworlds—Eon, Jad, and Felis—were far away. She ran a gloved hand along the stone wall beside her. Beautiful buildings rose on all sides—structures made of glossy stones of various natural shades, with veins of gold running through them. The doorways were all elegant arches and the windows were large. In the distance, beautiful mountains rose up, high above the small town, and several narrow waterfalls spilled off the sides of the peaks. When she'd landed her small stealth ship outside of the town, she'd made note of lots of rivers and lush meadows.

Lara pulled in a deep breath. The air was crisp and chill. Winter was coming on Tholla.

As excited as she was to see the inside of Eon territory, the small knot in her gut reminded her why she was here.

Tholla was home to the Temple of Eschar—one of the first warriors who'd created the Eon Empire. And in that temple was a very valuable, sacred gem.

A gem she was here to steal.

She'd been blackmailed into carrying out this mission. She blew out a breath. Steal three sacred Eon gems. *No sweat*. She swallowed a groan. She absolutely couldn't fail, because her sister's freedom depended on Lara's success.

Oh, and she couldn't forget that this mission would

also help save Earth from a deadly invasion. *No pressure at all.*

Fucking Space Corps. Lara still couldn't believe they thought they could steal from the Eon in order to convince the warriors to help Earth repel the Kantos. It sounded like a dumb plan to her.

She shoved her anger down. She had no choice, so there was no point moaning about Space Corps doing this shit to her. Lara knew better than anyone how dangerous the insectoid Kantos were.

She was a special forces space marine. She'd had bloody confrontations with them too many times to count. The ravenous aliens had been poking at Earth for years, gearing up to swarm in and invade. Eating up Earth's resources and killing humans for food.

Lara's nose wrinkled. Yep, she hated the Kantos.

The Kantos had killed Lara's dad. The old, faded pain still stung. Lara had adored her father, who had also been a space marine. He and his death were the reasons she'd joined the Corps. That, and her mother's downward spiral into a bottle after his death. Lara's mother had essentially ignored her young daughters, and most of the responsibility for raising her sisters had fallen to Lara.

Romantic love. It was the galaxy's biggest con.

Lara had trained and worked hard to make the special forces team...which guaranteed her a chance to kick some scaly Kantos ass.

But then, five months ago, everything had gone to hell. Her younger sister, Eve, an experienced Space Corps sub-captain, had been framed for a crime she hadn't committed.

Her ship had faced off with the Kantos, and people had died. Eve had been forced to take the fall for an incompetent captain, who also happened to be the son of an admiral.

Lara's anger was an ugly burn. While Eve had spent the last few months rotting in a cell on a low-orbit prison, Lara and their youngest sister, Wren, had been making a lot of noise about the whole situation.

Lara would do *anything* to secure Eve's freedom.

Of course, when they'd offered her this thieving mission, they'd also sent Eve off on a fucking suicide operation. Earth really needed an alliance with the Eon—and their technology and superior military—and the Space Corps was going all-out to get the warriors' attention.

So, Eve was sent to abduct a formidable Eon war commander, and Lara was sent to steal the three jewels the Eon held most sacred.

Such a stupid idea. God, Lara didn't even know if Eve was still alive.

She paused, pressing a palm to the stone wall. *Please be okay, Eve.*

Lara straightened and turned on to another street, keeping her head lowered. The Eon were all taller than her, but by Earth standards, she was tall for a woman, so she thankfully didn't look completely out of place. She'd made sure to wear platform-style boots as well, which gave her a few extra inches.

But she did keep her face down. The Eon all looked quite similar, so she knew her features would stand out. She didn't have the distinct Eon eyes, which were black, with different colored filaments glowing through them—

blue, silver, green, purple, gold. And Eon hair was brown —ranging from tawny brown threaded with gold, to deep mahogany. There were no Eon with blonde or black hair. And Lara's hair, inherited from her Japanese grandmother, was as black as night.

Ahead, a larger crowd had gathered in an elegant square. Several beautifully carved statues decorated the space, and a number of food stalls had been erected on the far side of the gathering. She knew there was a festival happening to celebrate Eschar.

Lara had already stolen two of the jewels—the gems of Ston and Alqin. The experimental stealth ship that the Space Corps had given her had worked like a charm. She'd slipped into Eon space, snuck right under Eon patrols, and landed on several planets, all without being detected.

Two gems down, one to go. She crossed the street to blend into the crowd. It wasn't far to the temple. Hopefully, everyone would be too busy out here with the party to notice her sneaking in.

Then she felt a prickle along the back of her neck.

Fuck. She dropped her head further and ducked into an arched doorway. Stepping back into the shadows, she peered around the edge of her hood and scanned the crowd.

He was here somewhere.

At the last temple, she'd been sneaking in when she'd run into an Eon warrior sent to hunt her down.

Lara smiled. She'd left him shaking from the electric shock of her StrikeBolt. But as she'd left, he'd promised that she'd feel his breath on the back of her neck.

He wasn't wrong.

The entire journey to Tholla, she knew he was coming for her. She'd felt it in her bones.

She looked around the square again. No sign of the huge, muscled warrior.

Pushing out of the doorway, she picked up her pace, winding her way through the crowd. The prickles kept increasing.

There. The spires of the temple rose up above the other buildings. Not far now.

Then the crowd parted.

And there he was, striding toward her.

Shit. Damn. Fuck. He wore all black. Not his black-scale armor—which the alien symbiont circling his thick wrist could generate for him. Instead, he wore a uniform of tight, black pants, and a sleeveless shirt that bared his huge biceps. Like most Eon men, he wore his hair long, brushing his square jaw, and it was a rich, chestnut brown.

He was too far away for her to see his eyes, but she knew they were black with strands of bright silver.

He stared at her across the square. The air charged. She felt his fury wash over her like a wave. She'd learned that the helian symbionts that Eon warriors were bonded to as a child amplified their emotions so that people around them could feel it.

Okay, Plan B.

Run.

Lara spun and broke into a sprint.

She darted through the square, bumping into a few

people, her cloak flaring out behind her. Startled cries echoed behind her, and she knew he was coming.

She turned a corner, arms pumping, and raced down the street. There were fewer people here, so she was able to easily dodge them.

Risking a glance back, she saw he was closing in. Her pulse spiked. His face was set like stone.

She watched a group milling on the path, blocking his way. He didn't slow down. Hell, he was going to mow right into them.

In a brilliant show of strength, the warrior leaped over the peoples' heads, landing on the other side without pause. He kept coming after Lara, not even breaking his stride.

Shit. Jerking sideways, she turned down a narrow alleyway. Like the rest of the town, the alley was clean and tidy, the stones beneath her feet shiny. She turned again.

Her chest expanded. The temple sat at the end of this street. A grand set of sweeping steps leading up to the huge, carved, double doors.

There were also a number of guards standing outside the doors. Way more than at the last two temples. Hmm, it looked like the warrior chasing her wasn't all brawn, after all. He'd clearly ramped up patrols, knowing that she was coming for the gem.

Lara smiled grimly. *It won't stop me, warrior.*

She heard the thunder of his boots behind her. Time to do what he wouldn't expect. She turned into another street, leading away from the temple. Pushing hard for speed, her lungs started to burn. But Lara ran to keep fit and enjoyed stretching herself. She pushed through the pain.

Lifting her head, she scanned the rooftops. She had an idea. She stopped, then leaped up and caught a window frame. Then she climbed.

Faster, Lara. She jumped across to the next window and climbed higher, her cloak tangling around her legs. Another leap, and she was at the uppermost set of windows.

Move it. Her hunter was coming, and she couldn't let him see where she'd gone.

She ascended smoothly. She went climbing with her sister Eve whenever their vacations aligned. Her sister loved it, and could climb like a damn monkey.

Lara curled her fingers over the edge of the roof and heaved herself up. She lowered to her belly, laying flat and staying low.

Now she just had to calm her racing heart. She knew the helian symbiont enhanced an Eon warrior's senses. She wasn't sure what the range was, but she didn't want her hunter tracking her down because her heart was thumping like a drum.

She breathed slowly in and out. *In. Out.*

Footsteps. She stilled. They slowed, and carefully Lara pulled a small device off her belt. She edged the tiny flexible camera over the lip of the roof. She looked at the small screen to see what was happening below.

The warrior stood in the empty street, his hands on his hips.

He was right below her hiding place.

He looked around and cursed. Thanks to the Space

Corps, Lara had a translator implanted behind her ear. She knew *Cren* was an Eon curse word.

The hunter circled around the street, then shook his head. He spun, striding away. Damn, the man could move. His long legs ate up the ground. He was like a big cat on the prowl. And she had a damn good view of a mighty delicious ass.

Shame he wanted to wring her neck.

Lara waited until she was sure he was gone. The sun had set, and night was well and truly settling over Tholla. She rose and walked along the roof. On the opposite side of the building, she dropped down to the street with a soft thump.

Then she turned and headed for the temple. She wasn't going to let extra guards stop her. She *always* achieved her mission.

Especially when the stakes were personal and so high.

She moved slowly and cautiously. She didn't want to stick out in any way. Ruling out an approach via the front door, she circled around one of the temple's protective outer courtyard walls.

Nearby, she heard talking and laughter. More people had come out to celebrate the goddess. No, not a goddess. Eschar had been a warrior.

Pausing, Lara looked up at the temple tower spearing into the night sky. It was part of the temple's defensive outer wall. It spiraled upward, and was made of a dark rock, veined with red. The tower looked pretty, almost delicate.

She pulled her HookWinch grappling device off her belt, and aimed it upward. She fired.

The line whizzed into the night and hit stone. She tested the rope, touched the device, and then she zoomed upward. The wind blew in her face, trying to pull her hair from its ponytail.

When her palms hit the stone wall of the tower, she climbed over the railing and onto the top of the structure. She turned and paused, her lips parting in awe.

A giant moon was rising over the horizon, bathing the town in silver light. It looked like something out of a fantasy movie. In the distance, the mountain range continued on as far as she could see, the many peaks glimmering as they were touched with moonlight. The view was gorgeous. It really was a beautiful moon, and she wished she was here for a different reason.

Then she tore her gaze away from the scenery and looked down. The temple courtyard was laid out below her, leading up to the main structure. A fountain burbled musically, somewhere close by. Green vines grew all over the stone walls and were covered in large, blood-red flowers. Red was Eschar's color.

The same color as the gem she was here to steal.

Lara drew in a breath of crisp, night air. *Okay, an angry warrior to evade, and a sacred gem to steal. Time to go.*

She started climbing down into the courtyard.

CAZE VANN-JAD LOCKED down his anger.

His helian pulsed. *I know. I know.* The Terran had escaped him. *Again.*

If Caze's father—a highly decorated Eon warrior—ever heard of this, he wouldn't be happy. *Cren,* Caze wasn't happy. He'd been raised to believe in the might of the Eon Empire and its warriors. And he'd been led to believe that Terrans were weak and inferior.

This invader was forcing him to rethink his beliefs.

As he strode down the street of Tholla's main town, he breathed deep, trying to pick up the woman's scent. She had a unique smell, richer and sweeter than he would have guessed. A picture of her formed in his mind —a long, athletic body that possessed curves as well. He'd definitely noticed the rounded hips and full breasts. Eon women were not curvy, so he found the difference intriguing.

Annoyed at himself for thinking of her body, he thought of her face. She looked like her sister, with a straight nose, stubborn jaw, and pointed chin. Eve Traynor was now mated to Caze's war commander, Davion. Like Eve, Lara Traynor had blue eyes, although hers were shades lighter than Eve's, with a dark ring around the outside.

Caze reached the front of the Temple of Eschar and strode up the steps. He nodded at the guards that he'd assigned there earlier. They opened the doors to let him in.

Right now, he needed to focus on protecting the gem. She'd come for it. Then he needed to capture her and retrieve the other two gems she'd already stolen.

And try not to kill her. He'd promised Eve that he wouldn't hurt her sister.

By Ston's sword, Caze could not believe that Davion —the fiercest war commander in the Eon fleet—had mated with a Terran.

Stepping into the temple courtyard, the lush scent of flowering blooms hit him. He scowled. The scent clogged his senses. As he strode across the inner courtyard, chimes danced in the wind somewhere nearby, making a pretty noise.

He strode through a huge, arched doorway and into the inner sanctum. Here, large, blood-red banners draped the stone walls, depicting images of Eschar in battle. Oval-shaped lights on the walls emitted a low, golden glow.

In the center of the space was a statue of the warrior herself, and the red gem that carried her name.

Eschar's Heart rested on the statue's chest.

Lara already had the gems of Ston and Alqin. She couldn't have this one.

As Caze stared at the red jewel, something dark moved within it. A symbiont. A helian, like the one that lived, attached to his wrist.

He took a step closer, then froze.

A scent reached him. A crisp, floral fragrance that wasn't lush and overpowering like the flowers. This one was sharper and sweeter.

She was here.

Caze turned his head, spotting no sign of her in the shadows. "Come out, Terran," he murmured.

There was only the sound of the distant wind chimes in response.

He moved closer to the statue. He'd find her and—

She hit him from behind.

Caze bent his legs, reaching back to grab her. But she shoved him and spun out of his reach.

She wore a long Eon cloak of deep gray over her sleek black-and-white space suit. He saw her pull something out of one of her many pouches and pockets. She shook it, and it extended into a sturdy-looking staff. A weapon.

With merely a thought, he called on his symbiont. Black scales spilled from his wrist, flowing up his arm. The armor rolled down his chest, covering his body. Then a glowing, silver staff formed on his arm. He closed his fingers around the smooth surface and lifted it.

He launched himself at his prey, and she sprinted to meet him.

Their staffs hit with a sharp *crack*. He shifted back and she came at him hard, staff whirling.

Cren, she was good. Caze had thought Terrans were incapable of discipline and strategy, let alone being able to meet an Eon warrior blow for blow.

Thwack. The staff hit his chest and he spun, dancing with her across the stones.

She raced toward a wall, put a foot to it, and flipped over his head. She landed close to the statue of Eschar.

He cursed. She reached out and plucked the gem off the statue.

"You aren't leaving with that," he growled.

She glanced over her shoulder. "Watch me."

Suddenly, she threw a small, metallic device at him. It sailed through the air and he recognized it instantly.

It hit his chest, prongs digging into him. Electricity skated over his body.

The Terran grinned at him. Caze stared back.

This time, he didn't drop, nor was he in pain and frozen by the electric shock.

Her grin faded and Caze felt the corner of his mouth quirk up.

"How?" she demanded.

"I came prepared. I have a device that nullifies the electric field of yours. I learn from my mistakes, Terran."

"My name is Lara."

"I know."

She tilted her head, considering him. "So, you aren't just a big, unintelligent beefcake."

"Beefcake?"

"Stud muffin. Muscleman. Hot stuff."

Caze growled. He didn't understand the Terran words, but he knew she was insulting him. "My name is Caze Vann-Jad."

She tilted her head. "I kinda like stud muffin."

Anger swept through him. She ignited his temper faster than anyone he knew. He wasn't used to feeling all his emotions storming out of his control. He was known for being ice-cold at work and on a mission. He'd been one of the best stealth operatives in the Eon fleet.

This rude, bold woman infuriated him.

She smiled at him.

And she was beautiful.

What? No. Where the *cren* did that come from?

Fighting off the strange thoughts, Caze launched at her again.

They fought their way across the room, and when his staff hit across her stomach, he heard the air rush out of her. She bent over and he reached out and snatched the jewel from her hand.

She straightened, lifting her staff, and scowled at him.

Then she moved fast, that deadly staff swinging. He swung his to meet it, the sounds of the two weapons smacking together filling the space.

She kicked out, and her boot slammed into Caze's knee. He grunted, his leg going out from under him. He felt the brush of her body and she snatched the jewel back.

"How do you like that?" She laughed.

The sound should have been grating, but her laugh was deep and melodious, and it hit him low in his gut.

Again, the reaction annoyed him. With a growl, Caze threw himself upward, charging at her.

She stumbled back, her boot catching on an uneven paver. When he knocked the staff from her hands, her eyes widened. The weapon clattered onto the stones.

Caze advanced on her. When her back hit the wall, he saw her face harden. She reached out and gripped one of the wall banners in her hand.

Before he knew what she had planned, she leaped into the air. Right at Caze.

By Alqin's axe. She spun her body, slamming into his chest, and whipped the banner around his neck. She pulled it tight, and as they both crashed to the ground, the fabric cut off his air.

She scrambled behind him, pulling hard.

Cren. Caze coughed, fighting to rip the banner away and breathe.

He tugged hard, finding a little slack. But she grunted, yanking back on it harder.

"Don't worry, warrior." Her voice was strained. She was putting all her effort into holding the banner in place. "I won't kill you. But once you're out cold, I'm out of here."

"Eve...*Desteron*," Caze forced out.

He sensed the woman choking him thinking. Then she snorted. "Right. If my sister is on your warship, she's probably in a cell, being tortured."

"No. Ambassa...dor."

Lara snorted again. "No way. Now I know you're lying. My sister is *not* diplomatic material. She's more likely to punch someone in the face."

"Mated... War commander." Caze coughed. His lungs were hurting and his vision was blurring.

Lara let out a wild laugh. "No way. An Eon warrior and a Terran? Yeah, right. Besides, just like me, Eve doesn't believe in love."

"Me...either."

He felt her lips brush his ear. "Then we do have something in common after all, Caze Vann-Jad."

Caze couldn't breathe. His body sagged and he crashed to the ground. The Terran was a warm weight at his back. He reached out clumsily and managed to get a hand on her ankle.

The lack of oxygen was making him punchy and, instead of yanking on her, he stroked her leg.

"Pretty. Strong." His voice was a husky whisper.

She stilled. He stroked her again.

"You aren't too shabby yourself, hot stuff."

But then she gave another tug on the banner around his throat and his vision blurred. Caze felt fingers brush his jaw, like a caress. *No. That couldn't be right.*

Boots stepped in front of him, and under the gray cloak, he saw the form-fitting black-and-white spacesuit slicked over her body. He looked up and their gazes met.

They stared at each other for a humming second.

Then she swiveled and, with a flap of her cloak, she was gone.

With the gem of Eschar.

By Ston's sword. Caze fought to draw in air. She might have won this fight, but he was *not* letting her get away.

CHAPTER TWO

L ara walked swiftly through the crowd. Lights had been strung up across the square, all glowing red, and somewhere, someone had started playing music. The haunting strings and trumpets filled the air.

On any other day, Lara would have liked to take her time—taste the food, smell the flowers, enjoy the music.

Most of her life consisted of missions and training. When she did have time off, she liked to indulge in all the sensual things she missed out on. She watched a group of Eon standing nearby, laughing. She'd always figured the Eon were stuffy and militaristic, but here, they seemed like regular people—laughing, dancing, and celebrating their festival. These Eon also didn't have a symbiont— only the warriors who were part of the Eon fleet had them.

The gem of Eschar was heavy in her pocket. She wondered if the warrior had recovered.

Nope, not thinking of him, or his silver-and-black eyes, or his big, hard body. Excitement winged through her. She had all three gems now. She could ensure Eve's freedom, and give Space Corps the leverage they needed to negotiate with the Eon.

She picked up speed. She needed to get back to her ship and off this planet before her angry hunter tracked her down again. Of course, she was taking a long, circuitous route back to where she'd hidden her ship. She couldn't risk him tracking her to it.

One of the revelers bumped into her. "By Eschar's grace, forgive me."

Lara lowered her head and waved a hand. She felt the man's curious gaze on her. Hurrying on, she pulled the cloak tighter around herself.

Suddenly, fireworks exploded overhead. The crowd erupted with gasps and exclamations.

Lara glanced up, watching the colors burst across the night sky. *Oh, wow.* Unlike fireworks back home, these danced through the sky, changing colors and creating fascinating shapes—people, mountains, animals.

Then she felt that damn prickle again.

She looked over her shoulder and her body locked. *Oh, shit.* Caze was running toward her at full speed, his big body moving fast but silently.

Lara spun and broke into a run. She sprinted through the crowd, shoving several people aside, ignoring their startled cries. She shot down a side street.

She couldn't hear him, but she knew he was coming.

The street ended at another square. This one held a crowd as well, but no music. It was dotted with stone-carved benches that invited people to sit and relax.

She dodged around the first one, then the second.

People were starting to pay attention to her. She risked a glance back and watched Caze leap over a bench.

Hell. At the next bench—this one thankfully empty— she pressed one hand to the stone, and leaped over it.

Faster, Lara. Her chest burned as she ran.

She reached a set of steps leading out of the square. She took them three at a time, then jumped over the handrail. She hit the ground, rolled, and came back onto her feet. She pumped her arms. *Faster. Faster.*

Another glance back. He was still chasing her. He leaped from the top of the stairs, powered through the air, and landed at the bottom with a bend of his muscular legs.

Her pulse hammered. He was a damn machine.

She hit another crowd of festival-goers, ducking and weaving through them. More fireworks exploded overhead.

Suddenly, Caze fell from the sky, landing in front of her. *Shit.* Lara pivoted to the side. His fingers caught the edge of her cloak and he yanked.

The cloak tore off her.

Shit. Sharp gasps came from all around and people stared at her. In her fitted spacesuit, it was clear she wasn't Eon.

Ignoring the attention, she put on a burst of speed, shoving through a line of people.

Nearby, a large, vine-covered tower speared into the sky. She ran straight toward it and jumped. Her gloved hands closed on the vines and she started pulling herself up.

A big hand wrapped around her ankle.

Dammit. Lara kicked and heard the warrior grunt.

His grip loosened and she pulled herself free. She scrambled upward, and reached the top of a solid-stone wall that snaked away from the tower. She climbed onto the wall and stood, getting her balance. Then she started walking across it.

"Nowhere to go, Terran. I want the gem."

He was up on the wall, following behind her.

"Not today, warrior."

"And you're coming with me."

She laughed. "My mission isn't over."

"I'll take you to Eve."

Lara was tempted. She wanted to believe more than anything that Eve was safe aboard an Eon warship. But she couldn't trust this man she didn't know. It could all be an elaborate ruse to lure her in.

She judged the distance to the end of the wall. Too far. He'd catch her. She pulled her backup staff off her belt. She was still pissed at him that she'd had to abandon her first one. It had been her favorite.

She turned to face him, shaking her staff out to its full length.

The big warrior smiled. "I was hoping you'd fight." His silver, glowing staff formed on his arm.

Damn, she really wished she had a symbiont that could make weapons for her.

Both of them gripping their weapons, they walked toward each other on the wall.

Lara swung. *Thwack.*

She drove him back a step, then he came at her. *Thwack. Thwack. Thwack.*

Shit, he was strong. She fought to keep her balance on the wall, moving back several steps. *Screw this*. She bent her legs, and using her speed, drove her staff upward into his.

This time, she managed to get him to move back a few steps. Then he ducked down, swiping out with his staff. She jumped it.

Lara brought her staff down.

He cursed and leaped backward. She charged at him. *Hit. Swing. Hit.*

She gritted her teeth, absorbing the power of his hits as she got in her own. Her blood was singing. She loved a challenge, and there was nothing she liked better than a good fight.

More fireworks burst overhead. She swung hard, with all her strength. Her staff slammed into his chest. He wobbled and Lara grinned.

He regained his footing and glared at her. She waggled her fingers at him in reply.

Caze came at her in a rush of strength and fury.

Shit. She barely avoided the end of his staff, and when she was off balance, he kicked one long leg at her.

She jumped and landed. "Sneaky."

"When I need to be. Give me the jewels."

Lara pretended to consider. "Nope."

Thwack. Their staffs hit and she pulled back, twirled it, and swung again. *Thwack*. He shoved forward, swinging his staff in a blur. *Thwack*.

Lara smiled as they fought. "Come on, hot stuff. That all you got?"

CAZE WONDERED how he could be infuriated and admire the woman's grit at the same time.

Lara came at him again. *By Ston's sword*, she had incredible balance. His helian throbbed. It was enjoying this.

He put more power into his blows and pushed her back. He swiped at her with his staff again and she jumped up with a laugh.

She was enjoying herself as well.

Her boots landed on the wall and she was already committed to her next hit. Her staff hit his arm, knocking him off balance. *Cren.*

He went down on one knee, balanced precariously on top of the wall. When he looked up, she winked at him, and then somersaulted over his head. He swiveled to look over his shoulder, watching her land with perfect precision.

He'd underestimated this Terran too many times.

"It's been fun, warrior, but I need to go." She yanked what looked like a blaster out of a holster. She aimed it at a building across the street.

Caze was already rising as a line whizzed out of the weapon, anchoring to the far wall, high above their heads.

Cren. He lunged for her.

She jumped. He watched her swing off the wall, sailing through the air. She whizzed downward, and landed on the ground below with a slight skid of her boots.

She retracted her grappling device, then looked up at

him and tossed him a jaunty wave. *Impudent woman.* He watched her run down a side street.

"Oh no, you don't." Caze turned and stepped off the wall.

He dropped straight down, then his boots hit the street. He crouched, one palm touching the ground, his helian absorbing the brunt of the impact.

Then he rose and ran after her, pumping his arms.

He wasn't letting her get away.

What about the gem? He scowled at his inner thoughts. That too, of course.

Caze darted through the twisting streets. He lost sight of her a few times, but her scent was strong, and he followed it.

He burst out of a street, and realized he'd reached the end of town. She'd run into the surrounding forest.

He smiled. "Keep running, my wily Terran."

His helian picked up her trail—that rich, feminine scent—and he followed. He pushed through the trees, trying to stay as silent as he could.

Soon, he heard her ahead of him. He smiled.

Then, she cried out, the sound sharp in the darkness. Frowning, he picked up speed. There were no dangerous predators on Tholla, but the small planet did have some poisonous plant life.

He broke into a clearing, and his steps slowed.

Lara was stuck in a large web spread between two trees. She twisted wildly, the near-translucent substance holding her tight.

Caze stopped, his lips quirking. He watched her struggle, and in the back of his mind, he wondered what in the name of Eschar had made the web. There were no spiders large enough on Tholla to create this. Nothing native, at least. It looked almost like a Kantos creation. He glanced at the sky. But there was no way there could be Kantos here, so deep in Eon territory. No Kantos had ever been this close to the Eon homeworlds.

Lara spotted him and cursed.

Still, this Terran had made it here undetected. He walked closer. "What are you going to do now, Terran?"

"Screw you."

"Your struggles are winding you up tighter."

She stilled. "What the hell is this?"

Caze frowned, studying the substance. "I don't know." He felt a trickle of unease.

"Cut me free," she demanded.

He crossed his arms over his chest. "Why would I do that?"

She cursed again.

He reached out, gripping her hip with one hand. She froze, her eyes narrowing on him.

He curled his fingers around her, going for her belt and where he'd seen her stash the gem. But the feel of her scattered his thoughts. She was firm but round at the same time, and so intriguing.

She sucked in a breath and he met her gaze.

Then he clenched his fingers on her belt. The pouch there was empty. He skimmed his hands down her sides, bending down on one knee to pat down her legs.

She made a choked noise.

He glanced up at her, looking up her long body. She had strong, toned legs, and as he skimmed his hands back up, she twisted. He knew that if she hadn't been stuck, she would have kicked him.

Caze straightened. That was when he noticed the bulge in the top of her suit, between the curves of her breasts.

He found the fastening at her neck, and started to lower it. Her blue eyes spat fire.

"You wouldn't have caught me if it wasn't for this damn web. You got lucky."

"I would have caught you."

"No way."

Her suit parted, and Caze hissed out a breath, his body going rock solid. He stared at her bare breasts. She wasn't wearing any sort of support beneath her suit. His body responded instantly, his cock hardening.

Cren. No. He ruthlessly controlled his reaction. Or tried to. He forced his gaze off her curves and onto the red jewel nestled between her breasts.

He reached in and his fingers brushed the side of her breast. They both groaned.

He looked into her beautiful, blue eyes.

"Don't get too excited warrior. I like sex and it's been a while. Despite you being a pain in my ass, you're big and strong." Her gaze dropped, sliding down his body. "I like big and strong, so it's nothing personal."

Under her bold gaze, Caze felt another surge of fierce desire. His cock was throbbing hard.

"Nothing personal," he repeated. "Your body is... different compared to Eon women."

He plucked the gem out and quickly did her suit back up.

Suddenly, there was the roar of sound overhead and a rush of downdraft. It set his hair dancing around his face.

Caze looked up.

Right at two Kantos swarm ships hovering above them.

"Oh, hell," Lara bit out.

Caze growled.

CHAPTER THREE

Lara recognized the ships. Kantos.

Shit. Hell. Fuck.

"How can there be Kantos ships here?" she said. "Wouldn't your Eon ships have blown them out of the sky?"

"I assume, like you, they've been experimenting with increased stealth capabilities," Caze said darkly.

Several figures leaped out of the swarm ships, diving down towards the trees. Streamlined wings flared out from their backs to slow their dive.

A Kantos kill squad.

Beside her, a flash of silver lit the dimness, and she turned her head. Caze's giant-ass sword glowed in the shadows.

He cut the web, freeing her legs. Her feet hit the ground, and with another slash, her arms were free.

There was another roar overhead, and when she looked up, she saw two Eon ships arrive, their lights spearing through the night.

The Kantos ships looked like insects, and the Eon ships couldn't be more different. They were black, sleek, and streamlined, glowing with blue lights. Instantly, the swarm ships fled, and the Eon ships gave chase. Laser fire lit up the night sky.

But Lara was well aware that the Kantos soldiers were already on the ground.

Lara reached for her hips and drew her twin blasters. "How many?"

"Six." Caze lifted his sword, scanning the trees. "Five soldiers and a bug."

"That's all?" She looked at the trees. "I'm insulted."

The warrior shot her an unreadable glance. At that moment, two Kantos soldiers slunk out of the trees.

Their bodies were covered with a hard, brown shell. They walked on four long, jointed legs, and held two razor-sharp arms up in front of their strong torsos. Their shoulders were covered in armored plates, and four small, glowing, yellow eyes dominated their ugly faces, right above a small mouth filled with sharp teeth.

Clicking filled the air, and she knew they were communicating. Her hands tightened on her blasters.

"Bet I can kill more than you, warrior."

Caze shot her an incredulous look. "Woman, I'm a trained Eon warrior."

She ran her tongue over her teeth. "So?"

Lara raced across the clearing, firing her blasters at the Kantos.

Lasers weren't effective weapons to use on aliens with a hard shell covering their body...unless you knew where their weak spots were.

She skidded to the ground, firing up at their bellies.

The clicking went wild and green blood splattered the ground.

She rolled back to her feet, aiming for the four beady eyes of the closest Kantos. He screeched and stumbled, crashing to the ground. *One down.* The other soldier shifted, holding his arms up to shield his face. But he was leaking green blood.

She grabbed several throwing stars off her belt. She'd sharpened them herself, and their edges could slice through a Kantos carapace. She tossed them in quick succession.

The first star hit the soldier in his narrow mouth, and the second followed. The alien made a choking sound, staggered, and hit a tree.

Two down. Lara strode forward, firing her blasters at the soldiers to ensure they were both dead.

She turned, checking the charge on her blasters. "That's two for me, warrior."

He stood there, just staring at her. He looked at the two Kantos bodies, then back at her again. The air charged with something, his mood pulsing off him.

But the warrior wasn't angry.

Aw, hell. Lara felt an answering tug of desire. She'd never had a man watch her fight and kill and get turned on by it.

She hadn't lied when she'd told him that she liked a hot, strong, and sexy male in her bed. She liked to ride a lover hard, but finding a man who liked everything about her: her strength, abilities, and take-charge attitude, was pretty damn rare.

Despite his icy façade, Caze was one fine male specimen.

But he was also an Eon warrior. The man sent to hunt her down.

All of a sudden, more Kantos burst into the clearing. Clicking filled the air and Lara tensed.

This time, it was Caze who charged.

Wow, the man could move. She watched him power into the aliens like a tornado.

For a moment, Lara was shocked. All she could do was watch him.

God. He was raw power. His sword moved so fast it was a blur of silver. He was like a dark storm making landfall and hitting hard.

One Kantos reared back, missing two legs. The remaining two Kantos attacked Caze together, their sharp arms swinging like swords.

Caze ducked and weaved, moving like a boxer. Then he turned and ran his sword through one of the soldier's guts.

The other Kantos slammed his arm down on Caze's back. He barely reacted, his armor clearly absorbing most of the blow. He spun, his gaze zeroing in on the last soldier.

The Kantos circled him, eyes glowing. And that's when Lara spotted the Kantos bug creeping up behind Caze.

Cowards. No way.

Lara strode toward the ant-like bug, which stood about waist-high. It was black, with two long antennae waving back and forth on top of its head, and green poison dripping from its pincers. She reached up over her shoulder and pulled her sword from the spine sheath running along the center of her back.

Her sword wasn't fancy. It was solid, made from the strongest metal alloy on Earth, and perfectly balanced for her.

She attacked.

With a vicious screech, the bug swiveled. It skittered to the side, dodging her swings.

Come on, Mr. Creepy-Crawly. She kept rushing the bug, driving it away from Caze.

Then she ran, leaped into the air, and somersaulted. She landed on the bug's back. It screeched and she bent her knees to keep her balance. She swung her sword.

Two of the creature's legs sliced off. It tilted like it was drunk and she leaped off. Turning mid-air, she slashed with her sword.

Two more legs were gone and its wild shriek made her wince.

It dragged its body across the ground in a desperate attempt to flee. Lara calmly advanced and raised her sword. With a hard swing, she decapitated the alien.

Green blood gushed and she jumped back. She turned in time to see Caze land a powerful blow to the last Kantos soldier. The alien collapsed in a pile.

She met the warrior's silver-black gaze.

"Three kills each," she said.

"More are coming."

There were always more Kantos. That was what made them so dangerous. They swarmed in, and used their greater numbers to annihilate other races.

Exactly what they had planned for Earth.

Through the trees, Lara heard more clicking.

She stepped up beside Caze, and they stood shoulder to shoulder as more Kantos emerged.

———

THE WOMAN COULD FIGHT.

It seemed humans had adapted and learned to use their strengths to battle the Kantos. Maybe there was more to Terrans than Caze had guessed.

Give us the gem.

The deep, raspy voice echoed in Caze's head. He eyed the Kantos elite, the leader of this group of fighters. He was a little taller, his shell a little paler, than the others. He could also speak telepathically in the heads of other species.

"Screw you, Creepy," Lara shouted.

As more Kantos soldiers came at them, Caze watched her swing her deadly sword. It was a simple design, but made of some reinforced metal. It had clearly been designed just for her.

Caze ensured he stayed out of her way as she spun the wicked weapon. But when she dodged back from the soldiers, he moved in. His helian pulsed, and he slashed with his sword, taking down a soldier.

He and Lara fell into a rhythm, cutting down several Kantos in a row.

"I've got one more than you now," she yelled.

Caze shook his head as she ran at the remaining aliens.

She pressed a boot to a stump of a rotted-out tree and leaped into the air. She landed on the back of a soldier, driving her sword deep and working it through the hard shell.

You will die here. We will take the gems.

Caze ignored the rasping mental voice. There was no way he was letting the Kantos take anything.

"Blah, blah," Lara said. "I'm evil and I'm going to destroy the world." With a quick flash of her sword, she sliced the head off the Kantos elite. "I'm really ahead of you now, warrior."

She leaped away from the body.

Caze scowled. He'd never met a woman like her. He straightened, rushing at the remaining soldiers.

But with their leader killed, the soldiers lost their cohesiveness. Working with Lara, Caze easily tore through the last of the Kantos.

Caze lowered his sword and pulled in a breath. He watched her clean green blood off her sword.

She glanced his way. "We're not a bad team, warrior."

"My name is Caze, Terran."

"And mine is Lara." Then she smiled. "I still killed one more than you." She paused and frowned. "They were after the gem."

Yes. And Caze wanted to know why.

But for now, his gaze was on the woman warrior staring at him, her chest rising and falling, drawing his attention to her full breasts. They were cupped by her spacesuit, but he knew exactly what they looked like.

He let his gaze drift over her. Everything about her enticed him.

She took a step closer, her own bold gaze sliding down his body. She lifted her head and their gazes clashed.

"You want to kiss me," she said.

So direct. He wasn't used to it. "I want to strip you naked, pin you to a tree, and thrust my cock inside you."

She jolted and her lips parted. "I think that's the most I've heard you say in one sentence."

They strode toward each other, closing the gap between them. Desire thrummed through Caze's blood, and he felt it in the air around them.

Some part of his brain shouted that she was his prey, his mission, but he ignored it. She pressed a hand to his chest and he retracted his armor.

"That is so cool," she breathed, watching the black scales flow off his body.

Her hand pressed against his black shirt, her fingers kneading his skin.

Caze breathed in her scent—healthy sweat and that familiar floral. It wasn't what he expected on such a seasoned fighter. Did she rub lotion on her skin? Or was it a special perfume she dabbed in sensitive places?

Under the practical spacesuit, he knew she was pure woman.

He lowered his head and heard her blow out a breath.

"You feel too damn good," she murmured.

"You smell good."

"This is crazy. You've been hunting me. We've been fighting each other."

"Yes."

His lips touched hers and he nipped at her. The taste

of her hit him. Then, with a moan, she rose up, and wrapped an arm around his neck.

Caze cupped the back of her head and deepened the kiss, sliding his tongue inside her mouth. *By Eschar*, she tasted so good.

Her tongue met his, stroke for stroke. She tasted good, smelled good, and need exploded in his gut.

He wrapped an arm around her, pulling her closer. She rubbed that gorgeous, strong body against him.

Then he felt a sting at his neck. He jerked.

What the Cren? He pulled back and he saw regret in her eyes.

"Sorry, warrior. That was a hell of a kiss, and I'm sorry to end it."

Caze's legs turned to water and he dropped. Lara supported him down until his knees touched the dirt.

Cren. She'd fooled him and injected him with some sort of sedative. He could feel the drug working through his system. His helian moved to neutralize it, but for the moment, he couldn't move.

His father would be furious that he'd let anyone best him, especially a Terran female.

Lara plucked the gem of Eschar from his pocket.

"I am truly sorry," she said. "But there is too much at stake."

"Lara—" His tongue felt thick, making it hard to talk.

She closed her eyes for a second, then she opened them. She rubbed her thumb over his lips, then bent her head and kissed him.

Caze couldn't move his arms. All he could do was growl in frustration.

"Sorry, babe." She rose, cast one last glance at him, then jogged into the trees.

He lost sight of her, and managed to throw his head back and roar.

CHAPTER FOUR

L ara snuck back into the town. It was risky, but she needed to mask her scent trail and this was what Caze would least expect of her. Plus, it was now the most direct route back to her ship.

There were warriors everywhere, all wearing symbiont armor.

She blew out a breath. She knew they weren't looking for her, they were searching for the Kantos, but the last thing she needed to do was draw any attention to herself.

Sticking to the shadows, she moved along a wall. Some colorful fabric hangings had been pinned up for the festival, and she quickly snatched one down. She whipped it over her head, covering her dark hair and obscuring her face.

She hurried through the streets. The gem was nestled once more in her suit. It felt like it was burning against her skin.

She licked her lips. And tasted Caze.

Her belly tightened. *Hell*. She'd kissed the warrior.

She'd liked it. She'd practically climbed his big body. His big, hard body.

Focus, Lara, or you'll get your ass caught.

Soon, she came out on the other side of the town without incident. Her stealth ship was hidden up in the hills nearby. Overhead, two bright moons filled the night sky, as well as the orb of the planet Ath.

Trying not to move too quickly, she ducked across the final street and into a grassy field. She moved up a hill and into the trees. By moonlight, she found a small stream and followed it. After a while, she was far enough from the town that she flipped on the flashlight attached to the shoulder of her suit.

There. She spotted the large tree with sprawling branches where she'd left her ship.

She hit a control on her belt and there was a shimmer in the night. The holographic camouflage dropped.

The stealth ship was tiny. It only fit two people, and was made purely for speed and secrecy. She pressed her palm to the door lock and it slid open. She climbed into the tight confines.

She quickly opened a reinforced panel on one side wall. Inside, was a sturdy, black case. She flipped open the lid and her chest tightened. The two gems she'd stolen were nestled in black foam. The seafoam-colored gem of Ston and the bright-blue gem of Alqin. Pulling out the red gem of Eschar, she settled it into the remaining space.

Then she closed the lid and replaced the panel.

"I'm coming, Eve." Lara sat in the pilot seat and the console flared to life. She touched the controls. She needed to get off this planet before an enraged warrior came looking for her.

She worried a little about there being extra Eon ships in the air, chasing down the Kantos. But hopefully they'd be too busy and with her stealth mode up, she should be able to sneak off the planet undetected.

She palmed the controls...but the engines remained silent.

What the hell? She coded in the launch sequence again. Nothing.

"Engines are not responding," the computer said in a modulated voice.

Great, just what she needed. "Run a diagnostic."

"Cannot comply."

"Why not?" Lara bit out.

"Cannot comply."

She slapped her palms against the console. Of all the times for her to have engine trouble. *Why me?* "Computer, check fuel levels."

"Fuel at optimum levels."

"Fuck." That meant there was something wrong with the engine. She pushed out of the seat, and went to a built-in storage cabinet. Inside, she found the maintenance tool kit and scanner. She pulled them out.

Moving outside, she aimed her flashlight at the hull, and dropped the tool kit on the ground. She opened the engine panel at the back of the ship.

Everything looked fine to her, but she was a special forces marine. She could fight, kill, and subdue, but when it came to engines, she sucked. She knew dick-all about machinery and fixing it.

"Problem?"

The deep voice turned her blood to ice. She turned her head.

Caze leaned against the side of her ship, his big, brawny arms crossed over his chest.

She straightened. "You did this!"

He raised a brow. "I disabled your ship, yes. I found it before I came looking for you."

"Dammit." Lara kicked the side of the ship, but she really wanted to kick him.

"Point to me," he said.

She narrowed her gaze on him. His face was impassive, but she was certain the warrior was feeling smug. "I left you sedated, so I'd say we're even."

The silver in his dark eyes flashed. "Not even close, Lara Traynor."

SHE DIDN'T HAVE a helian amplifying her emotions, but Caze had no trouble detecting the anger pumping off Lara.

He was the one who should be mad. She kept getting the drop on him, and she'd left him sedated in the middle of a forest overrun with Kantos.

But instead, he found himself admiring her. He certainly wouldn't underestimate her again.

She huffed out a breath. "So, you sabotaged my ship?"

"Yes."

Her nose wrinkled.

"You don't need to do this, Lara." He pushed away from the hull of her ship. "Earth has recalled you from your mission. I can take you to Eve, and she can confirm it."

Lara stared at him, eyes narrowed.

She was so distrusting. She reminded Caze of himself.

"I can't trust you," she said. "You just want the gems back, and to lock me up."

"Then trust your sister." He lifted his arm, tilting the screen on his wrist so she could see it. "Watch."

Eve's face filled the screen. The sisters looked alike, but comparing them now, he saw Eve's face was a little narrower than Lara's.

Lara grabbed his wrist. "Eve."

"It's a recording."

"Lara, if Caze finds you, you can trust him," Eve said. "Mostly."

Caze frowned at the woman's words.

Lara laughed.

"He won't lie to you," Eve continued. "But he is a badass warrior. If he hurts you..."

Lara snorted. "As if."

For the first time in his life, Caze felt the urge to roll his eyes.

"I survived my mission, Lara. I successfully abducted War Commander Thann-Eon." A smile flirted around the edges of Eve's mouth. "Then the Kantos attacked us. Dav and I crash landed on a planet."

Lara's brows rose. "Dav?"

"The Kantos were hunting us, and we were forced to work together."

"Sounds familiar," Lara mumbled.

Eve smiled again. "And then I fell in love with my magnificent war commander."

Lara gasped. "What the—?"

"We're mated now, Lara." A pause. "I know you and I have never believed in love, but Lara—" Eve shook her head, her face glowing "—when it's right, it's the best damn thing in the galaxy."

Lara snorted. What a load of crap.

"We're back on the *Desteron*, and the Eon king has made me ambassador to Earth." Eve wrinkled her nose. "He wants his gems back, Lara. Trust Caze, and bring the gems to me."

Lara looked at Caze, then back at the screen.

"There's something else," Eve said. And even Caze could detect the woman's anger through the recording. "The Space Corps didn't just blackmail you and me into these crazy missions." Eve dragged in a breath. "They did the same to Wren, as well."

"What?" Lara exploded. "No way."

"They sent her to hijack an Eon warship, the *Rengard*." Eve shook her head. "She succeeded. But I've got no idea where she or the ship are now."

"Fucking hell." Lara turned and punched the side of her ship. "Wren."

"Come to me, Lara. I'll see you soon." Eve lifted a hand, like she was going to reach through the screen to touch her sister. Then the recording ended.

Caze watched Lara pace by her ship. "Wren is your sister."

"Our baby sister. She isn't military trained! She couldn't fight a flea."

Caze wasn't sure what a flea was, but it didn't sound very challenging.

"The recording didn't look doctored." Lara stopped and shot him a suspicious look.

He crossed his arms over his chest. "Eon warriors do not engage in subterfuge."

"She didn't look under duress."

"I can assure you, she's happily mated to the war commander." Caze still found that incredulous. An Eon and a Terran. And Eve could command Davion's helian, something that was unheard of in Eon history. "They are in love."

Lara wrinkled her nose, just like her sister had. "Love is for fools. And Eve is *not* a fool."

"I agree with you on both counts. Love is a weak, useless emotion. But she and Davion do appear to care for each other."

"He's a good man?"

"The best. The best warrior I know."

Lara blew out a breath. "God, they dragged my baby sister into this as well. Fucking Space Corps. Wren is a computer geek for God's sake."

"She's clearly as tough and determined as her sisters if she succeeded in hijacking an Eon warship full of warriors."

Lara's face paled. "Dammit, if they've hurt her…"

Yes, the sisters were very devoted to each other and

very similar—extremely protective. But Caze couldn't give Lara any assurances. War Commander Malax Dann-Jad of the *Rengard* was a formidable warrior.

"Come back with me," Caze said. "The best way to help your younger sister is to meet with Eve and then find Wren together."

Lara sighed and then nodded. "Okay, warrior, I am reluctantly going to trust you."

Elation filled him. "Get what you need from your ship, including the gems. I'll arrange for the ship to be secured."

She pointed a finger at him. "Betray me, and I'll slit your throat."

"You can try, Terran. Now, hurry. We'll take my ship back to the *Desteron*."

With another nod, she ducked inside. He watched through the doorway as she grabbed a backpack and shoved some belongings into it.

"I wish you'd listened to me at the Temple of Alqin," he said. It would have saved them a lot of time...and bruises.

She snorted. "You said that you'd come for me, and I'd feel your breath on the back of my neck as you hunted me to the end of the galaxy. Not a good way to make me trust you."

Caze grunted. He'd never been known for his diplomacy or tact.

Lara ducked out of the ship and grinned. "Besides, fighting you was fun."

"You are a unique woman, Lara Traynor."

"Thanks. I *think* that was a compliment." She waved a hand forward. "Now, lead the way."

He turned, retracing the path back to the town. "I'm glad you trust me now."

"Not an inch, warrior. One wrong move, and I won't hesitate to take you down."

Caze felt that appreciation again. "The gems." He held out a hand. "Give them to me for safekeeping."

"Not a chance." She tightened the strap on her backpack.

He'd figured as much. But as long as she was with him, he could help her keep the gems safe until they returned to the *Desteron*.

They walked in silence and it was almost companionable. He led her around the edge of town. The streets were far emptier now, with more warriors patrolling. The surprise visit from the Kantos had left the locals cautious.

The Kantos. What the Cren did they want with the sacred gems of the warriors?

Caze led Lara to a small docking area. The guards at the gates bowed their heads to him and he nodded. Inside, there were a small number of Eon ships. His stealth ship was at the end, larger than Lara's and far more streamlined.

"Ooh." She stroked the black, metal hull. It had a faint scale pattern embedded in it.

Caze watched her hand and wondered if she'd ever looked at a man in the hungry way she eyed his ship.

He shook his head, forcing himself to focus on the mission. He led her inside.

"I can stow your pack."

He got a dry look. "No, thanks."

They both settled into seats in the cockpit. It was angled at the front, with an angular viewscreen in front of them.

Caze started the prelaunch sequence, watching as Lara struggled with the slightly-too-large harness. He reached over to help her buckle it and as soon as he touched her, electricity arced between them.

He quickly sat back. "Ready?"

"Ready."

He communicated with the docking controllers, then initiated takeoff, and the ship lifted. He saw her lean forward, still cradling her backpack. They zoomed into the night sky and minutes later, they broke the moon's atmosphere and arrowed into space.

"It will take several hours to reach the *Desteron*," he told her.

She nodded, her fingers gripping the console in front of her. Then she lifted her hand. "What's this?"

There was something sticky on them.

Caze frowned. *By Alqin's axe.* His muscles tensed and he called on his symbiont, opening his senses.

He sensed...something.

Something that was trying very hard to hide itself.

Suddenly, there was a noise behind them, and they both swiveled. The floor panels of his ship burst open, and a Kantos bug erupted out of the floor.

CHAPTER FIVE

W*ell, fuck.*
Lara leaped up, staring at the Kantos, her hands going for her blasters. But she couldn't use the lasers. Not on the ship.

The creature was red and black, and covered in a light fuzz. It had a bulging thorax, and six skinny, black legs. It opened its mouth and sprayed poison.

Shit. Caze burst into action, slamming into Lara and driving her to the floor.

She heard metal sizzling as it melted.

"Off." She shoved at him.

Then she heard clicking noises. Dammit, there were soldiers in here, as well.

Surrender. Give us the gems.

At the mental voice, Caze growled.

"That's a hell no, bug face." Lara turned her head to look up at Caze. "Ready?"

He raised a brow. "Ready."

They both surged up.

Lara reached over her shoulder and pulled her sword. A silver glow filled the space as Caze's sword formed on his arm.

They moved together, slashing and swinging.

Caze slammed his boot down, pinning one of the bug's thin legs. It screeched.

"Lara!" he roared.

She swung her sword down, stabbing at the Kantos' red body. Her sword hit, and the creature writhed. She shoved with all her strength through the hard shell and her blade sank deep. With another screech, it slumped to the floor, poison oozing out of it.

"Soldiers," Caze shouted.

"Go high," she yelled.

They both swiveled. The Kantos soldiers were charging at them, but Caze and Lara were ready. The ship's lights flashed off their swords. Lara gritted her teeth and slashed. It was challenging to fight in the tight confines of the ship, forcing her to keep her swings short and sharp.

Caze sliced an arm off one soldier. Another flash of silver, and the other arm was gone as well. The soldier shrieked, writhing around.

"Down," Caze called.

She automatically ducked, and his sword sliced over her head. As it cut into the other soldier, Lara swung low. Her blade hacked into the soldier's legs.

The Kantos tilted and collapsed.

Lara spotted something that the alien was holding in one claw.

Her gut cramped. Was it a grenade?

The soldier that was already on the ground surged up, and Caze rammed into him like a football player. The soldier crashed into the console so hard that the metal dented.

The other soldier tossed what he was holding.

"Caze! Look out!"

The warrior spun. They watched the object sail into the air and stop, hovering.

What the—? Lara's chest hitched. It was a small winged insect.

The creature was no bigger than her hand, and had pretty, translucent wings that glistened pink and purple in the light.

It danced around, leaving a faint mist in the air.

Lassitude flowed through Lara and she blinked. A smile broke out on her lips. She felt so good, so relaxed.

Warmth flowed through her, and she lowered her sword, her arms dangling by her side.

"Lara," Caze called out.

"It's all okay, warrior. Everything is great."

He surged toward her, then stopped. He shook his head like he was trying to clear it, then he looked up and smiled.

She grinned at him. "Oh, God, you should do that more often."

"What?"

She pressed her hands to his hard chest. "Smile. You're damn handsome when you do."

"I've had no reason to smile." He reached out and touched her hair. "Until now."

A clicking noise filled the air.

They turned their heads and watched as an elite Kantos rose up out of the hole in the floor.

Lara blinked and felt a tickle in her head. "I feel like...I should be concerned."

Caze pressed a hand to his head. "This is wrong."

The elite burst forward, raising its sharp arms. It moved around them, searching the ship. It yanked open cabinet doors.

Where are the gems?

The raspy voice in her head made her wince. No, this wasn't right.

Caze made a choked sound. "Never...tell you."

The elite swung an arm and it slammed into Caze's head. The warrior dropped like an imploded building.

No. Lara gasped, the pleasure clouding her head dimming.

The elite snatched the flying bug from the air. Instantly, Lara's head cleared.

Dread and fear filled her throat. *Shit.* They'd been drugged or hypnotized or something.

Caze lay face down on the floor, not moving. Her belly went hard. The elite stared at her with its burning yellow eyes.

Where are the gems?

Shit, her backpack was lying on the floor near the console. She forced herself not to look at it. Tried hard. But her head was foggy, a strange compulsion flooding her system. She glanced at the pack.

The elite's eyes flared. *Thank you, Terran.*

Shit. "You should have kept me high and strung out,

bug boy." Lara lifted her sword and launched herself at the alien.

CAZE'S HEAD THROBBED. The unforgiving pain made nausea wash over him. He opened his eyes and everything was a blur.

He heard the sound of fighting and turned his head. His vision cleared.

Lara was fighting an elite.

He watched as she was rammed into the wall of his ship. The elite swung an arm at her and she ducked. Metal crunched and she countered, slicing out with her sword. It slashed across the alien's hard chest.

Caze tried to move, to push himself up and help. But his body wouldn't respond.

His helian was working overtime to heal him. He knew he had some sort of head wound.

Lara wasn't moving like she usually did. She was sluggish, slow. Then he remembered the flying insect.

Cren. They'd been drugged.

The elite caught Lara with one arm, pinning her by her neck to the wall. She twisted, fighting him, but his other arm whipped out. It opened up a slash across her thigh.

Lara cried out, her body slumping.

The Kantos released her. As she fell, he landed a hard blow to the back of her head and she collapsed to the floor.

No.

The elite stared down at her dispassionately. Then he turned and snatched up her backpack.

Curses ran through Caze's head. Again, he fought to move, but his body didn't respond.

The Kantos used one of his clawed hands to rifle through the backpack. He pulled out the three Eon gems.

Then the creature looked at the viewscreen, and although his expression didn't change, Caze sensed the alien's satisfaction.

Using everything he had, Caze managed to lift his head. A large, raider-class Kantos cruiser filled the viewscreen. It was on an intercept course.

Caze sucked in a breath. There was nothing he could do right now. He needed to heal, and he needed to protect Lara.

When the time was right, they could try to escape.

Clang.

They were docking with the Kantos ship.

The elite moved, gliding on his four legs. He started making a clicking sound, and Caze heard the beat of multiple Kantos feet.

They'd been boarded.

A second later, something gripped Caze's ankle, and he was dragged along the floor. He saw another soldier appear and grab Lara by the back of her suit. He dragged her toward the door.

Caze kept his eyes slitted, pretending to be unconscious. He felt someone slap something on his helian. *Cren.* More of that black ooze that blocked his ability to communicate and command his symbiont.

Then his body bumped across the ground as he and

Lara were dragged off his ship and onto the Kantos cruiser.

He hadn't checked in with Davion and the *Desteron* yet. When he missed the communication time, Davion would know something was wrong.

But who knew where he and Lara would be by then.

Caze saw a glimpse of dark-brown walls, and the ugly scent of rotting things.

His face was close to Lara's, and he saw the blood staining her hair. He ground his teeth together, hoping she was okay.

The Kantos would pay. He'd make them all pay for this.

CHAPTER SIX

L ara woke with a thumping headache. *What the hell? Did she have a hangover?*

She opened her eyes and froze. Nope, no hangover. The place looked unfamiliar, but it smelled like Kantos.

The walls were a dark brown, reminding her of tough Kantos shells, and had a faint hexagonal pattern. The floor beneath her felt sticky.

She'd been on a Kantos cruiser once during an extraction mission, and this looked similar.

Turning her head, she realized she was resting against something hard and warm. She looked up, taking in the long thigh she was using as a pillow.

Caze. He was in a seated position against the wall, his arms chained above his head. Her pulse leaped.

"Caze?" She carefully shifted up, cupping his cheek.

His eyes opened. They were unfocused.

"I'm sorry, father. I failed you. I've dishonored your training."

She frowned. *What the hell?* There was so much disappointment in his voice.

"Hey, Caze? It's Lara."

He blinked and slowly his eyes focused on her face.

"Lara."

"That's right. You okay?"

He nodded. "My helian is trying to repair my wounds, but the Kantos disabled it, so it isn't working at its full ability. You?" His gaze went to her head.

Lara lifted a hand to the back of her head, felt dried blood and a lump. "This?" She waved a dismissive hand. "I've had *way* worse before."

His lips twitched. "Or you have a very hard head."

"Don't make me hurt you, warrior." She touched her belt, hoping to find the antidote to the helian restraint. Space Corps had managed to get their hands on some of it.

Nothing. She bit back a curse. They'd cleaned out her gear and weapons.

"Your thigh?" Caze asked. "The elite cut you."

Lara moved her leg and saw the nasty puncture. "I'll live and it isn't bleeding anymore." Hopefully she didn't catch anything nasty.

She reached up and tested his chains. Then she stood, gripped them, and pressed one boot to the wall. She pulled and tugged. They wouldn't budge.

"Go, Lara," Caze said. "Get off this ship and get help."

"And leave you to be tortured and killed?"

"You've been fighting and running from me for days. What do you care?"

She lifted a hand, reaching into her hair. "I've decided I sort of like you."

"Sort of?"

She cocked a hip. "You're still a big, alpha-male pain in my butt."

He made a choked sound. "And you are a maddening woman."

"Yep." She slipped a small lock pick from her hair. Then she leaned forward, slipping it into the lock on the chain.

Caze made a strange sound and she looked down. Her breasts were pressed against his face.

Oops. "Sorry."

That black-and-silver gaze flicked up. The silver filaments burned brightly. Lara felt a very inappropriate rush of desire between her legs.

"Don't be." His voice was low and husky.

Click. The lock released, and one of his arms was free. She dropped the chains and moved to his other arm.

Finally, she picked the second lock, and he was free.

When Caze stood, he grabbed her, yanking her into his chest. For just a second, Lara let herself lean on him.

"Thanks," he murmured.

"Don't mention it." She cleared her throat. "So, we need a plan. I don't have any of the symbiont antidote. They took it."

He nodded. "We'll find some. Our first priority is to locate the gems. And then we get off this ship."

"Okay." She stepped back. "But we have no weapons."

"We'll pick up something along the way."

They headed to the cell door. "Then let's do this."

She watched as he pried open the door, his muscles flexing. They ducked their heads out, peering into an empty corridor. The roof was arched, the walls dark brown, with patches of glowing amber in places.

A faint hum echoed through the place. Creepy.

Caze waved her out and they snuck down the corridor, staying close to one wall. At one spot, thick, gold fluid dripped down the wall, and they carefully avoided it.

Ugh. She just didn't want to know.

"The labs should be on the lower level," Caze said, softly. "That's likely where they're keeping the gems."

Lara nodded. She glanced down the corridor. Ahead, a ramp descended deeper into the ship. She picked up speed. "Keep up, warrior."

———

THEY MOVED STEALTHILY DOWN the ramp to the lower levels. Lara was good. She moved like a spirit, quiet as the wind.

Reaching the bottom, Caze paused, listening for any sounds or movements. With his helian trapped, his enhanced senses were muffled. *Cren.*

They moved into another long corridor. They hadn't gone far when clicking echoed ahead of them.

"Soldiers," he murmured.

"There." She nodded toward a side corridor.

They ducked around the corner, and Caze pressed

her close to the wall. The click of Kantos' footsteps echoed loudly as several soldiers passed by.

He waited until he was sure they were gone, then lifted his hand and pointed. Lara nodded. They moved out and continued down the hall.

An open doorway loomed ahead, a wide arch framed in a bone-like substance. Caze paused and peered inside.

A lab. Or, at least, the Kantos version of one.

Long benches filled the space, each covered in a multitude of strange and unusual items. Some he could identify, and some he couldn't. Several oval-shaped vessels were filled with liquids of varying browns and blacks. Other objects looked like eggs. They pulsed gently. The walls were covered in small cocoons, attached in a haphazard pattern.

Thankfully, the lab was empty of any Kantos.

"Caze," Lara whispered.

He followed the direction of her gaze and spotted two vats of bright-orange fluid.

The antidote.

They hurried over and Lara lifted the lid. Caze plunged his wrist in.

Instantly, the black ooze trapping his helian dissolved. He pulled his arm back out and black scales moved up his arm. They flowed across his chest and then down his body until his entire big body was encased in organic armor.

He let out a relieved breath. His helian pulsed, happy to be free.

"I don't think I'll ever get tired of watching that," Lara murmured.

"Search the rest of the lab for any sign of the gems."

They moved up and down the benches.

"No sign of them," she muttered.

Cren. "Let's try the next lab."

Lara shifted, bumping into a bench. It scraped against the floor, and a vat of black liquid teetered on the edge.

"Shit." She caught it, and gently pushed it back onto the bench. "Sorry." Then she went still. "Caze. Look."

Beneath where the vat had been sitting was a depression in the bench. And resting inside the cavity was a pale-green jewel.

The gem of Ston.

He shifted closer and lifted it carefully. Inside the stone, a black shadow moved. A proto-symbiont. He carefully placed the gem in his pocket.

"One down," Lara said. "We'd better check under the other containers."

They searched quickly. The other gems weren't there.

Lara lifted a short, sturdy length of metal pipe. She tested its weight. "It's no sword, but this works for me."

Caze nodded toward the door, but as they neared it, he heard Kantos clicking sounds. *Cren.*

"Hide."

He dived in behind a bench near the side wall, leaning in close to some equipment. Lara squeezed in beside him. They shifted around and Caze yanked her into his lap.

The noises intensified. The Kantos were in the lab.

Caze tightened his hold on Lara and moved his head

slightly. He could see the four dark legs of a Kantos close by.

He hoped they didn't notice the missing gem. He listened to things clanking, objects being moved, and things being placed on different benches. Caze tried to keep his breathing slow and steady.

He turned his head and his nose brushed Lara's. Heat flared in her gaze and his body tightened.

Her breath puffed over his lips and he fought his body's intense reaction. Now wasn't the time. He never let anything distract him from a mission, ever.

She bit her lip and his gaze dropped. Heat suffused him. That mouth. Despite the situation, he couldn't stop himself. It was crazy and he didn't care. He leaned forward and touched his lips to hers.

The loud sound of something slamming on a bench pulled him back to the present and Caze jerked. Movement caught his eye, and then the room went silent.

The Kantos had left the lab.

Caze cleared his throat. "We need to go."

Lara nodded and rose. They moved to the lab door and she quickly peeked out. "Clear. There's another doorway not far down the hall."

He hoped the other two gems were close. They started down the corridor, and he saw three doorways ahead. They glanced into the first.

Lara lifted a hand, four fingers held up. Sure enough, there were four Kantos working in the lab, moving between the benches. Caze scanned the space. There was no obvious sign of the remaining gems. They silently snuck past.

He pointed to the next doorway. That one was empty, and a quick search didn't uncover any more gems.

"Caze." At her harsh whisper, he saw her waving from the next doorway.

He looked inside and his muscles tensed. The gem of Alqin was suspended in a tank of clear liquid.

They entered quietly.

"How do we get it out?" she asked.

Caze studied the tank for a second, then he made a fist, and smacked it into the side of the tank. It cracked, and fluid flowed out onto the floor.

He reached in and grabbed the jewel. He turned and handed it to Lara. "You hold on to this one."

She nodded, opening her suit enough to stow it inside. "No more labs. Where's the gem of Eschar?"

"We'll need to search the rest of the ship."

But before they could leave, a group of Kantos soldiers walked into the lab. They froze, clearly shocked to see Caze and Lara.

"Shit," Lara muttered.

Violent clicking filled the air, and the soldiers moved toward Caze and Lara, yellow eyes focused on them.

Caze formed his sword and Lara lifted her pipe. She spun it around.

"I feel like beating up some creepy crawlies."

They rushed to meet the soldiers.

Caze swung his weapon, carving through the legs of the lead soldier. Beside him, Lara leaped onto a bench, sending things crashing. She jumped, her thighs clamping on a soldier's head. Her pipe crashed into the head of another soldier. Hard shell cracked under the blow.

Then she twisted, knocking the Kantos under her off his feet. She lifted the pipe again.

Bloodthirsty and unforgiving. *By Eschar*, she was a magnificent woman.

Caze pressed his lips together, and focused on bringing down the remaining soldiers. One Kantos landed a hard hit to Caze's chest and he went spinning into a bench. Glass smashed.

Lara appeared, her pipe slamming hard into Caze's attacker. It cracked against his teeth and he shrieked.

With a single blow, Caze finished the soldier.

There was one left. As Caze and Lara turned, the soldier took one look at them and ran out of the room.

"Fuck," Lara said.

Together, they sprinted to the door. As they hit the corridor, alarms started blaring.

Cren. Kantos reinforcements were coming.

"Looks like we'll have some company," Lara said.

They jogged down the corridor. "We need a place to hide."

Lara scanned the walls and pointed. "You think that's a maintenance conduit?"

There was the outline of a door in the brown wall opposite. Caze slammed his boot against it and it popped open.

Inside was a vertical tunnel with a ladder carved into the side. "Go."

Lara started climbing and Caze closed the door

behind them. The closed-in space smelled terrible and he heard Lara retch.

"Gah, I hate the smell of Kantos," she muttered.

"You'll dive into a fight with multiple Kantos, but you can't handle a tiny bad smell?"

"Bite me," she called back.

It occurred to Caze that the idea was actually something he wouldn't mind doing. He forced his thoughts back to the situation at hand.

The tunnel was dark. There was a faint gold glow emanating from the walls just barely letting them see. He set his boot to a foothold and followed Lara up.

You cannot escape. The guttural voice echoed in their heads.

Lara looked down and they shared a glance. He watched her grit her teeth and keep climbing.

We will find you.

"Yeah, yeah," Lara said.

They reached the end of the ladder. It was covered by a hatch, and Lara grunted as she opened it.

"Clear." She pulled herself out.

Caze followed. They were in another corridor. On this level, the walls were all made of a layered, web-like substance.

They stayed close to the wall, moving fast down the corridor.

As they turned a corner, they surprised a lone elite. Caze grabbed the alien's arms, yanking him around. The Kantos' legs scrabbled on the floor and Caze pinned him against the wall. He pressed an arm to the elite's throat.

"Where is the gem of Eschar?" Caze growled.

The Kantos thrashed. Caze formed a knife on his arm and the tip of the blade lengthened, pressing into the elite's hard skin. A thin trickle of green blood dripped down the Kantos' neck.

"The red gem." Caze shoved harder. "Where. Is. It?"

"Oh man, watching you being badass is hot, warrior."

The Kantos' gaze flicked to Lara, then back again. *Not on the ship. It was sent somewhere else.*

The words in his head made Caze snarl. "*Cren.*"

"He could be lying," Lara said.

Caze pressed harder and the soldier made a harsh noise. "You aren't lying to me, are you?"

The alien's legs thrashed. *No.*

Suddenly, a deafening, horrible screech echoed down the corridor, and the elite flinched.

"What the hell was that?" Lara looked over her shoulder.

But Caze was busy looking at the Kantos elite. Its golden eyes flickered, and Caze realized the alien was afraid.

The targ. They've released the targ.

Caze's blood turned to ice. "Lara, we need to go. Now!"

CHAPTER SEVEN

L ara and Caze jogged down the corridor. She glanced his way and saw his jaw was clenched tight.

"We need to find a ship and get off this cruiser," he said.

"What's a targ?"

He turned his head. "I've never seen one, but I've heard stories. They're a genetically engineered bug. The Kantos spliced the genetic material of a lot of different creatures together."

Great. "Okay."

"It's pure predator. A hunter, a killer. It can only think of swallowing anything in its path."

Swallowing? Her mouth went dry. "Sounds creepy."

They turned a corner, and another loud shriek echoed through the ship. It made her ears ring and the hairs on her arms lift.

Cautiously, they rounded another corner.

Caze scanned ahead. "We should be getting close to the swarm ship—"

He broke off and Lara sucked in a breath. A terrifyingly large creature lumbered into view at the end of the long corridor.

"*Cren*," muttered Caze.

It looked like...a blob.

The alien was a gray color, with several stubby legs below its bulbous body and a long tail that split into two pronged ends. They waved around behind it. A large, sucking mouth sat in the center of its mass. It didn't appear to have eyes, and it didn't have any fangs, either.

It actually didn't look so bad, really.

It let out another earsplitting shriek that made Lara wince.

Then it moved. Lightning fast. *Right at them.*

Oh, shit. Maybe it *was* worse than it looked.

Caze grabbed her arm and yanked her around.

"Run!"

They sprinted down the corridor. Behind them, the targ rushed to follow. It flowed along the floor.

As it got closer, Lara smelled it—rotting meat. *Ugh.* Her stomach rolled.

She glanced back. Dammit, it was gaining on them. They turned another corner. The next shriek was right behind them.

Suddenly, Caze rammed into Lara, knocking her sideways into another corridor.

"Where are we going?" she yelled.

"Wherever that thing isn't."

They both pumped their arms, and Lara sucked in air.

"We need to make it to the swarm ship hangar bay," he said.

The targ's tail slapped down between them. Caze slashed down with his arm and sliced into it. Green blood sprayed.

An angry shriek reverberated off the walls.

"You're making it angry, hot stuff."

"I think it's already angry."

There was another corridor ahead and they turned into it. Just in front of them, a group of Kantos soldiers stepped out of a doorway.

As Caze and Lara sprinted past them, she heard furious clicking from the soldiers.

She glanced back, just as the targ reached the soldiers.

Its dual tail wrapped around the soldiers, plucking them off the floor. The giant alien sucked them into its huge mouth, one after another.

The final soldier struggled and threw his limbs out. He gripped the sides of the mouth, stuck halfway into the huge, gaping maw.

Then the targ shrieked and the soldier was gulped inside.

Gross.

"It just ate a bunch of soldiers," she said. "But it's got no teeth."

"That's right. You dissolve in the acids in its gut. Slowly and painfully."

Double gross.

"Hangar is down the next corridor," Caze said.

They turned and skidded to a stop. A row of Kantos soldiers blocked the way, their sharp arms raised.

"*Cren.*"

"Warrior, this situation deserves a fuck."

They stood there, trapped. Then, she heard the targ round the corner behind them.

All the soldiers stiffened. A few took steps backward, looking ready to run.

Hold the line. The voice of the elite echoed in everyone's heads.

"Suggestions?" she asked.

The targ shrieked, flowing closer.

Give us the gems.

"No," Lara said. "Go fuck yourself."

In front of them, the Kantos soldiers moved closer. Behind them, the targ closed in, tail slapping against the floor and wall.

Caze and Lara were well and truly stuck in the middle.

On Caze's arm, his sword melted away and a large blaster took shape.

She hissed. "You can't shoot in here. You'll blow a hole in the ship, and we'll all be dead."

"You have a better idea?"

Think, Lara, think. She'd been in tight spots loads of times before. She looked up. There was a large grate in the ceiling above their heads. For ventilation or maintenance, maybe.

"There." She jerked her chin up.

Caze followed her motion and nodded. He jumped,

punching a fist through the grate, opening the hole. When he landed back down, he grabbed Lara and tossed her up through the opening.

Wasting no time, Lara heaved herself inside the narrow, horizontal tunnel. The flow of air told her it was for ventilation. She scrambled into the small space, just as Caze pulled himself in after her.

Down below, she heard a chaotic symphony of clicking and shrieking. *So long, suckers.*

"Let's move," Caze said.

They started to crawl. It was a damn tight fit for Caze's broad shoulders. Then there was a thump and Caze grunted.

She looked back and met his gaze. Suddenly, his body was dragged backward toward the opening.

"Caze!"

She swiveled around, cursing. She saw that one part of the targ's tail was wrapped around Caze's leg.

It was dragging him back down.

"No!" She grabbed Caze's arm, pulling.

"Go, Lara. It's too strong."

"Shut up."

He growled and she squeezed by him, her body pressed against his. She had no weapon, so she kicked at the tail. She kicked it again.

"You can't have him, asshole. He's kind of growing on me. He's grumpy, but he's pretty good in a fight."

Caze groaned. "Lara—"

"Shush." She gave another hard kick, grinding her boot into the gelatinous flesh. The tail loosened.

Then Caze was free.

He shoved himself forward, deeper into the tunnel. The tail waved around in front of Lara. It struck at her and she dodged to the side, ramming into the wall.

The grate cover that Caze had knocked into the vent tunnel was resting nearby. She snatched it up, and then rammed it into the tail. A muffled screech came from below. She used the grate like a shield, pushing against the creature.

Then she felt a warm chest press against her back. Brawny arms surrounded her, and Caze rested his hands beside hers on the grate covering. They pushed together.

Lara grunted, and the tail was driven back down toward the corridor below.

"A...little...more," she bit out.

She felt the brush of air on her ear, as Caze put all his strength into it. The covering got close to the hole, and then the strong magnets that usually held it in place clicked on.

Thump.

The covering dropped back into position over the hole, cutting the tip of the tail off. In the corridor below, there was an earsplitting shriek. The bit of amputated tail flopped around in the tunnel.

"Let's move, Lara. Fast."

She huffed out a breath. "I like that idea."

Caze gripped her hair and tugged her head back. His amazing eyes bored into hers, and she saw a tangled mix of need reflected in them.

"Kiss me, warrior."

With a groan, he pressed a hard, fast, and regrettably too short, kiss to her mouth.

"Thank you, Lara."

"Any time, hot stuff." Her voice was more than a little husky.

Then Caze urged her forward into the tunnel. "Now go."

———

CAZE STAYED CLOSE behind Lara as they scrambled down the vent tunnel.

She'd saved his life. Fearlessly. Without hesitation.

Now he planned to return the favor and get her off this ship.

"Faster," he said.

"Going as fast as I can, warrior."

A screech resonated from below them. *Cren.* The targ was tracking them.

By his best estimate, the main swarm ship hangar should be close. But with the targ hunting them, they might need a change of plan.

"Lara. Stop here."

She glanced back at him and he pointed upward. A vertical vent tunnel speared up right above their heads.

"You said the hangar was closer—"

"But so is the targ. There will be a smaller, secondary hangar one deck up."

She nodded. "Put more distance between us and it."

He urged her up. "Go."

She didn't argue. She squeezed by him and moved into the vertical tunnel. She pressed her boots to the wall and started shimmying up. It gave him a perfect view of her ass.

Caze blew out a breath. His friend Brack would laugh his head off at how easily distracted the great, icily-controlled Caze was on this mission.

He pressed his hands to the inside of the shaft and followed her. They moved quickly, and soon, Lara stopped by a grate.

"This is it." She pushed it open.

The opening led to a vast hangar filled with swarm ships. It was vertical, with the small ships clinging to the walls like insects. He looked down and couldn't see the bottom.

"We need to climb to the closest ship," he told her.

Lara nodded and pulled herself out. She clung to the wall for a second, then she moved downward.

A swarm ship was only a few arm-length's away. Caze followed.

The swarm ship had a rounded nose, and three tentacle-like protrusions at the back. On the hard, brown hull, Caze found a control panel. He commanded his helian, and a cable snaked out from his armor, meshing with the ship's controls. Then, he set to work hacking the system.

There was a series of low, screech-like beeps, and the side door of the ship slid open.

Lara grinned at him. "Nice job, hot stuff."

"I'm not sure I like this name you've given me."

Her grinned widened. "It suits you. But don't worry, I know your name, Caze."

He cupped her jaw. He felt something loosen in his chest, unfamiliar emotions blooming.

Suddenly, the targ tail smashed through the wall right beside them.

Cren. It wriggled around and smacked into Lara. With a sharp cry, she lost her grip and fell.

Caze lunged for her, grabbing her hand. He grasped her with one arm, holding her as she dangled over the bottomless hangar.

The tail wrapped around her middle.

"Dammit." With her free hand, she punched it.

Gritting his teeth, Caze pulled her up. The tail tightened around her middle and squeezed.

"Ow," she cried.

"Hold on, Lara. Grip onto the swarm ship with your legs."

She looked at him for a beat, then she swung her legs out. She circled them around a part of the ship. The second part of the targ tail broke through the hole in the hangar wall and clamped onto one of her legs.

"Caze—"

"Hang on." He formed his sword and sliced through the first tail.

It released her instantly. As it fell away, he saw that it had shredded her suit around her midriff. He saw flashes of her smooth skin.

He sliced through the second tail holding her leg. He heard a distant, enraged shriek.

"Let go of the ship," he said.

She did, swinging away from the ship, clinging tight to his hand. He pulled her up, retracting his sword. Then he reached out with his other hand.

When he got her close, he yanked her into his chest. She clung to him, panting.

She blew out a breath. "Thanks, warrior." Her voice was raspy, her face contorted with pain.

She was hurt. He looked down at her ruined suit. Her skin was bruised, as well as tinged a strange green color. Poison. *Cren.*

But there was nothing he could do until they were safely off the Kantos ship.

"Can you hold on?"

Her lips pressed together and she gave one decisive nod.

Any other woman Caze knew would be screaming in pain. He threaded his hand through hers and pulled her down toward the open door of the swarm ship.

They dropped inside. He saw she was moving gingerly, beads of sweat on her forehead.

The swarm ship was a similar size to his own stealth ship. It had been designed with the four-legged Kantos soldiers in mind. He did a thorough scan of the ship, ensuring there were no *Cren*-cursed Kantos waiting in ambush for them this time. He'd learned that lesson.

Lara collapsed into an over-large seat, and Caze took the one beside her. He grabbed her hand, and his helian-enhanced senses picked up her elevated pulse and shallow breathing.

"Hold on, *shara.*"

She let out a shuddering breath.

He touched the controls, his helian connecting with the ship. He managed to fire the engines and detach from the wall. He maneuvered them toward the exit at the bottom of the hangar. They had a dizzying view of the thousands of swarm ships clinging to the walls.

The ship wobbled slightly from side to side, but by the time they approached the large, circular, mouth-looking hangar door, he'd worked out the controls.

"It's not opening," Lara said.

Caze tried all the commands he could find. The hangar door remained closed, and they were zooming right toward it.

"Caze..."

He smiled grimly. Well, he knew of one way to get it open.

He found the weapons systems and fired.

Boom.

Lara jerked, and a huge ball of flames and debris expanded before it was sucked out into space. A trail of swarm ships was pulled off the wall, tumbling out uselessly into space.

Avoiding the debris, Caze flew them out the resized hangar door. As soon as he hit black, he quickly set course. Next up, he set his helian to work disrupting any tracking devices the Kantos had on the swarm ship.

He wanted them far away before the Kantos caught on and sent ships after them. And he wanted to ensure they had no trail to follow.

"We made it, my tough Terran." He glanced at her, and his stomach fell away.

Lara had passed out in the seat beside him.

CHAPTER EIGHT

L ara had never felt pain like this. It was like acid was eating her from the inside out.

"Lara. Lara."

She wanted to escape away from the agony and into the darkness. But the deep voice was calling her away from the dark and closer to the pain.

She felt hands on her and she swung out with one arm. Her fist connected with something hard.

A curse. She reluctantly opened her eyes.

She was flat on her back on the floor of a... Kantos swarm ship.

Hell.

Turning her head, her gaze locked with Caze's gorgeous eyes. Silver strands glowed, and he looked worried, even a little panicked.

Fire tore through her middle and she cried out.

"I know, *shara*. We'll get you healed."

"Hurts... Bad."

He stroked her hair. "I know. The targ has some sort

of poison on its tail. And it's broken the skin." Caze's fingers were touching her stomach.

She bit her lip to keep from crying out. She felt him grip her suit. Then he tore it down the middle.

Lara was in too much pain to care that she was practically naked. The suit had built-in support, so she wasn't wearing a bra. But Caze was focused on the wound on her belly. She felt him lift the gem from where she'd had it pressed against her skin.

He set it aside, barely paying it any attention.

"Hold on, Lara. We'll get you healed."

Another wave of pain hit her. Worse than before. She moaned, tears pricking in her eyes. Then she saw him hold something above her.

It was a small vial of red fluid. It glowed the same ruby color as the gem of Eschar. *Pretty.*

"Where...?" The pain made it too hard to talk.

"This is havv. A healing liquid infused with bio-organisms similar to my helian. I carry a small emergency vial in my boot." He squeezed the havv onto her belly.

Lara felt warmth, then fire.

She arched and screamed.

"Shh. I'm here. The healing will hurt, but the havv will work into the wounds and neutralize the poison. Then it will heal you up as good as new."

"Hurts."

"I know. I'm sorry, *shara.*"

He pulled her into his lap and Lara curled into him. No one had ever held her when she'd hurt before. As a child, her father had been dead and her mother had been off in a drunken haze. Lara, as the oldest sister, had been the one to tend to her sisters' booboos. She'd cradled them, hugged them, but no one had held her.

God, he was so warm and strong.

"Shh." He stroked her hair.

Lara felt dizzy now and the pain was making her feel sick. Her stomach twisted. "I'm going to be—"

Caze reacted quickly. He turned her to the side and some sort of container was shoved in front of her. Lara retched into it.

Once her stomach was empty, she slumped back against him. "Sorry."

"Don't be." He shifted her and pushed the container away. Then he held up a cloth, wiping her mouth. "I wish I had water, but I don't think we should risk ingesting anything on this ship."

She nodded, pressed her cheek to his chest, and closed her eyes.

"Rest." A big hand stroked her hair. "Let the havv work."

She nodded, and felt him lift her and rise to his feet. She dozed a little, and when she came to again, Caze was sitting in the pilot's chair, with her still held snuggled in his lap. Thankfully, her pain was now a dull throb.

She realized now that his chest was bare. He'd stripped his own black shirt off and slipped it over her.

A golden sensation glowed inside her. Swallowing, she turned her head to look at the viewscreen. Stars streamed past them outside.

"How long until we reach the *Desteron*?"

One of his hands squeezed her arm. "Too long. We

need to hole up somewhere. We both need some rest, and the Kantos will be searching for us."

Damn.

"I know a hidden Eon stealth station close by. It's used by the Empire's stealth agents."

He was worried about her and putting her wellbeing first. She reached up and stroked his cheek. "You're a nice guy, Caze Vann-Jad."

His gaze met hers. "No one has accused me of that before."

"Your secret is safe with me, warrior." She paused. "I bet your mom thinks you're nice."

"I didn't have a mother."

Lara frowned. "Huh?"

He shifted her, reaching out to touch the controls, his gaze scanning the screens. "For the Eon, only mated pairs are fertile, and mating is now a rare thing."

She tilted her head, her brow scrunching. "Why?"

"We don't know, we just know that rates have dropped over the decades. But many couples still marry and commit. Eon can apply to adopt children. Our scientists have a breeding program, using the best DNA from the brightest and most talented Eon."

"Wow," she murmured.

"My father raised me. He was a warrior, had spent his life in the Eon military. He wanted to pass on his skills." Caze looked down at her. "From the time I was young, he focused on my training, including fitness, hunting, weapons, strategy."

Now she frowned. "What about being a kid? Having fun?"

"That was not in my father's skill set."

She made a hissing sound. "Kids need more than skills, Caze."

She knew that better than anyone. In her grief, Mika Traynor had taught her daughters a hard lesson. She'd turned to alcohol, forgotten about her children, and finally gotten herself kicked out of the Space Corps.

Even now, so many years later, Lara felt a tightness in her chest remembering. She, Eve, and Wren had raised themselves, and a lot of the load had fallen on Lara. Sometimes there had been no food, or Eve would have no shoes for school, or the landlord would come banging on the door for overdue rent. But still, she'd had her sisters. They'd played, fought, and laughed.

Who had Caze had?

"It wasn't a bad upbringing, Lara," Caze said. "My father taught me a lot. He's an honorable man."

She made a non-committal sound. "You mentioned him. When we were trapped on that Kantos ship. You were sorry you disappointed him."

Caze's mouth snapped shut. "He...has always expected the best from me."

"Did he tend your wounds? Did he hug you? Did he make you laugh?"

A long pause. "Those are not things one gives to a warrior in training."

Her chin dropped to her chest and she felt some inexplicable emotion inside her. The need to show him there was more to life than being a stoic warrior. But hell, it wasn't like she was the best example of living life to the fullest.

"You're close to your sisters."

Caze's words weren't a question. "Yes. We fight occasionally. Eve and I had plenty of hair-pulling fights when we were younger, and quite vocal arguments as we got older. Our younger sister, Wren, would get upset and break us up. She was always the voice of reason, and the one to calm us down." Lara smiled. God, she missed them. "We love each other. We had to look out for each other."

He raised a brow in question.

Now Lara felt uncomfortable. She rarely talked about her childhood with anyone. But Caze had shared.

A spasm of pain hit her and she grimaced.

"Keep talking, Lara."

"You're just trying to distract me."

"Yes."

"See, a nice guy." She blew out a breath. "My dad died. He was a space marine and was killed in an early Kantos confrontation."

"I'm sorry, Lara."

"My mom...fell apart. She started drinking." Lara frowned. "Do the Eon drink? Alcohol?"

"Yes, we brew a liquor called Voga. I don't drink it."

"Of course, you don't."

"So, your mother was unable to cope with the loss of your father."

"Right. He was the love of her life and she blamed the Space Corps for his death. She was in the Corps as well, but as her drinking and wild conspiracy theories increased, she was discharged." Lost in old memories, Lara stared ahead. "It was like she'd forgotten that she had three little girls, who were also grieving for the father they'd lost. It taught me that love is a crappy thing. If love breaks you, it isn't worth it." She shook her head. "After she left the Corps, Mom took jobs to make ends meet... when she was sober. She was either away at night a lot working security, or at home, drunk, having spent our grocery money on booze. It was just me, Eve, and Wren. We did what we could to make sure we had food to eat and clothes to wear."

He stroked his hand down her side. "Your mother didn't do right by you."

"She was weak. Love made her weak." Lara's eyelids drooped. She was so tired.

"The healing tires your body. Sleep now."

She tensed. She'd be unconscious and vulnerable.

"I've got you," he murmured. "Sleep."

And Lara decided she did trust him. Strangely, she trusted this warrior sent to hunt her down. Who instead had protected her, saved her, and fought by her side.

Trusting him felt right. More right than anything in her life until now.

She closed her eyes and drifted off.

THEY WERE GETTING close to the stealth station. It was tucked behind a small moon, and hidden by the best camouflage generator the Eon had created.

Caze touched the controls. He'd be happy to be there and off this swarm ship.

In his lap, Lara stirred, and her blue eyes opened.

"Hi," he murmured.

"Hey." She straightened, her eyes heavy.

"How do you feel?"

"Pain feels better. I'd kill for a long, hot bath and something to eat."

"A side effect of the havv is hunger. Once we get to the station, I'll feed you. And I may be able to sort that bath out for you."

She smiled. "Really? I'd *love* a bubble bath. There's that nice guy again. I'd definitely owe you one, warrior."

"We're approaching the stealth station now."

She leaned forward, looking at the viewscreen. "I can't see anything."

Caze commanded his helian and it pulsed, sending out a signal. There was a shimmer in space directly in front of them.

A small space station appeared.

It was a multi-level, cylindrical structure that tapered to points at the ends. There was a docking hanger at the base, storage areas, and a small living area at the top. Stealth agents could use these stations to rest, recover, and restock.

He flew them in, and the hangar doors opened. Landing the swarm ship wasn't smooth, but soon, they were down. He parked the ship between two Eon stealth ships.

"Welcome to Skeo Station," the computer voice said.

"Come on." Caze helped Lara to her feet.

She was looking much better, but she still gripped his arm as he led her out of the ship.

"No one else is here?" she asked.

He shook his head. "These stations are unmanned."

Their boots echoed on the sleek floor as they crossed the hangar. The place was all metal and sparse lines.

"You guys don't believe in decoration, do you?"

Caze had never given it any thought before. They passed several storage rooms he knew held weapons and parts. He led her into the lift, and they zoomed upward smoothly.

The doors opened into a living area and Lara gasped. There were no windows, but a large screen dominated one wall. Right now, it was showing a display of pretty colors dancing together.

"See, decoration," he said dryly.

Her lips quirked. "I stand corrected."

The station had a functional kitchen area, and some long sofas grouped in the center of the living area.

"Bedrooms." He pointed to several closed doors. "And the washroom."

He opened the door. Lights clicked on, illuminating the shower stall. Then he pressed a button on the wall. The stall slid away into the wall, and a tub appeared from the floor.

Lara gasped. "That is incredibly cool."

"Space-saving and efficient." He touched the tub controls and water flowed into the tub. "You have a soak. It'll help with your recovery. I'll organize some food."

She ran a hand along the edge of the tub, pleasure on her face.

He touched a panel on the wall, and programmed it for some things to put in a bath. The synthesizer flared to life. Several salts and lotions appeared. Lara reached for them, sniffing the contents of each container, and closing her eyes to savor the smell.

Caze watched her face, unable to look away. She was a tough, battle-hardened soldier, but she also took time to savor and enjoy every small sensation.

When had he ever stopped to enjoy a taste, a smell, or a sensation? When had he ever done more than just be a perfect warrior?

She sniffed another container and moaned a little.

The sound made Caze's cock rise. "I'll bring you some new clothes." He hoped she didn't notice how husky his voice sounded.

As he turned to leave, she grabbed his arm. "Thanks, Caze. No one's ever looked after me before...thanks."

Warmth burst in his chest. He nodded. "You're welcome, Lara."

He closed the door behind him and, as he crossed to the kitchen, he thought more about the way Lara Traynor seemed to embrace life.

He felt deeply—for his work. But being around Lara made him realize that he kept everything else at bay—just like his father had taught him.

Even his fellow warriors.

A good warrior lets no one close. A good warrior has no liabilities or weaknesses. His father's deep voice echoed in his head.

And on Caze's rare nights with a woman, there was no intimacy, no time spent together doing anything else other than fucking. He fucked and left.

Annoyed with himself, he shook his head. Lara needed clothes and food. He changed directions and entered one of the bedrooms. In the closet, he found mostly black Eon uniforms. But he did find some casual clothes for use on the station. That included a smaller shirt the same color as Lara's blue eyes.

He knocked on the bathroom door. "I have clothes for you."

There was no response.

"Lara?" Had she had a relapse of her injury? Had she slipped under the water? "Lara?"

He was about to barge through the door when he heard her voice.

"Come in."

Caze opened the door and he stepped inside. His steps faltered.

She was in the tub, covered in a mound of bubbles. She'd pulled her hair up in a messy knot on top of her head. She shot him a lazy smile.

His gut contracted hard. Need hit him like a blow. He dropped the clothes on a small table near the bath.

"I'll find us some food." He spun and hurried out.

He moved across the living area, desire drumming through him. *Cren*. Desire for a Terran woman who had him twisted up in knots. His fingers clenched and he sucked in air.

Lara needed food. Focus on taking care of her, not your own desires.

He quickly ordered up some food and he methodically ate his own nutritional pack. He spent more time selecting some tasty Eon delights he thought Lara might like.

He liked the idea of watching her enjoy them.

He waited several minutes and all was quiet from the bathroom. Again, he felt that niggle of worry. She'd been badly injured. He needed to check on her.

He gave a small knock before he entered.

The bubbles were almost gone, and Lara was resting in the tub, her eyes closed and her beautiful body on display. His gaze moved over her full breasts, tipped with pink nipples.

"Lara?"

Her eyes opened. "Sorry. I must have dozed off."

He swallowed and held up the plate. "I have some food for you. The havv uses a lot of energy."

She sat up, her breasts sliding beneath the water. But he could still see them. He fought back his groan.

Moving closer, he crouched beside the tub. She reached for some of the food, studying it with interest. If he'd expected the strange food to make her hesitate, he was wrong.

"Um, that's good." She munched on some *gadd.* Then she reached for more.

Lara savored each tidbit, making small sounds that turned him on more. Caze was just a throbbing mass of desire. She made him tell her the name of each food, and he saw her cataloguing every taste and smell.

After trying some *telra* cakes, she licked her fingers with a long moan. He was sure his cock was going to burst out of his trousers any second. She sagged back in the water, clearly satisfied.

He wasn't satisfied. Not by any means.

Take care of her, Vann-Jad. Be a warrior.

"I should...check your injuries." *Cren*, his throat felt like it had an asteroid lodged in it.

She nodded, sliding an arm across her breasts.

Her stomach was clearly visible through the water. Caze leaned over the tub, sliding one hand into the water.

Focus on her injuries. He stroked new, pink skin. The havv had performed its job very well.

"It looks good." So good. Against his will, his eyes drifted down to the small tangle of black curls between her toned legs. He swallowed a groan.

"Caze."

He jerked his gaze back to her face. Her cheeks were flushed from the warm water. Except, as he looked at her, he wondered if it was just the water. Heat warmed her eyes.

"You can touch me," she murmured.

He sucked in a breath, just staring at her.

"I want you to touch me," she said.

He swallowed. "You were hurt—"

"I'm not hurt now." She reached for his hand and brought it up, placing it on her breast.

His fingers convulsed on her and she moaned. In his head, a voice told him to leave. Get up and get away from the temptation of this woman.

"Our mission—"

"Touch me."

His fingers moved, caressing the soft fullness of her. He moved his thumb over her nipple and she moaned. Seeing her response made him do it again, plucking at it. It pebbled for him.

She shifted in the water. "Yes. More."

He cupped her breast, stroking and savoring. He watched her face, listened to the noises she made. He wanted to know exactly what she liked. He let his hands move lower, over her flat, toned belly. Then he reached those intriguing curls between her legs.

Caze stroked his fingers through them, and she opened her legs for him. Her eyes were glittering, her lips parted. He slid one hand between her thighs, finding the soft folds there.

"Yes." Her hips bucked, water splashing.

Something inside him broke free. "You like that."

"Yes, Caze. I need it."

"You've been driving me crazy. You know that?"

She moaned. He stroked those beautiful folds again, then thrust two fingers inside her.

Lara cried out, her head dropping back. "So good. More."

"I'm in charge right now, Lara." She was so tight, her body clenching his fingers. So slick, so uninhibited. "You'll take what I give you."

He found the small nub with his thumb, rolling it. Small, husky cries escaped from her.

Hunger vibrated through him. His cock was hard and painful.

He reached into the bath and pulled her out of the water. She gave a small cry, gripping his shoulders. He lay her down on the mat beside the bath. He knelt between her legs, looking at the way her wet skin glistened.

"Lara, you're so beautiful."

She arched her body and she let her legs fall apart.

He shoved them wider.

"Look at you, spreading your legs for me."

His words made her gasp, her tongue licking her lips.

He dropped his head to her breasts, sucking a nipple deep. She made an incoherent sound, and with impatient need, he licked, sucked, and nipped at her plump breasts and pink nipples. With one last, hard suck, he let the nipple pop from his mouth.

He had to taste her. Was desperate for it. He wanted to hear her scream his name.

Caze lowered his head and put his mouth between her legs.

"Oh, yes." She shoved her hands into his hair, directing him. He nipped her thigh, and then his tongue was in her, tasting her. She rocked against his mouth.

By the warriors. He wanted to take his time, to savor, but the flavor of her burst in his mouth. More. He needed more. He wanted to devour.

"Harder, Caze. I want your tongue on my clit."

He loved that she knew what she wanted and was bold enough to demand it. Usually, he had to temper his strength when he was with a woman. They never asked for more. He obeyed, licking and sucking that intriguing nub. She cried out his name, grinding against his face.

Caze took his time, relishing her response. Her legs moved, wrapping around his head, her thighs clenching on him. He felt like a god, put here just to pleasure her.

He thrust his hips helplessly, his cock weeping against his trousers.

Her moans and cries got more desperate. He slid a finger inside her tight warmth and sucked her clit into his mouth. He worked a second finger inside her, driving deep. A second later, she exploded.

She cried his name again, her scream echoing off the walls, her thighs shaking around his head.

As she flopped back on the mat, Caze was a mass of roaring need. Air sawed in and out of his lungs.

Her blue eyes locked on him.

"Come here." She pulled him over her until he straddled her chest. Her hands were at his trousers, tearing them open.

Then her hands were on his cock.

Caze groaned. Sensation slammed into him.

She pumped him, and her fingers moved around the wide head of his cock, spreading the seeping fluid she found there.

His blood was pounding through his veins, and her caresses tore another groan from him.

Lara pulled him closer and lifted her head. She sucked his cock into her mouth.

"Lara." A tortured groan.

She started sucking him, hand sliding around his ass to pull him closer. It felt so good.

He thrust gently into her hot mouth. "Lara."

She licked him and he hissed. "Stop thinking, Caze. Just enjoy. I'm giving, and your job is just to take the pleasure."

She sucked him again, her cheeks hollowing as she put effort into it. Soon, he was thrusting his hips forward, and the sounds she made drove him on. Caze shouted several guttural obscenities.

Licking along his length, she looked at him with heated eyes. "You like that?"

"Yes. More."

She circled her tongue around the head of his cock. Then she sucked him deep, to the back of her throat.

He shouted. He'd never seen anything sexier. Never seen anything that had driven him to the edge like this.

She kept working him, and he suddenly felt fire rip down his spine.

"I'm going to come."

Her mouth slid off him with a pop. "So come, warrior. I want you to come on my skin, my breasts, my belly. Show me what you've got."

The sexy taunt threw him over the edge. With another harsh groan, he gripped his cock and started coming. Fluid hit her breasts. He shouted his release as he spilled over her skin.

Panting, Caze slowly came back to reality.

Lara was smiling at him, looking at where he'd marked her skin. She murmured his name, and he felt that single word deep inside him.

She raised her head and her smile widened. "Well, I think it's safe to say that we're both feeling *a lot* better."

A laugh broke from him.

CHAPTER NINE

A beeping noise came from the other room.

Lara heard Caze curse, his body tensing above hers. "That's an incoming call."

"Go." She waved at him.

He pushed off her and yanked his pants up. He gave her a long look, seeming reluctant to leave, then strode out.

Lara pressed a hand to her temple and blew out a breath. This was a dangerous path. Fooling around with an Eon warrior, and enjoying it...

Hell, loving every wild, sexy second of it.

She knew that Eon warriors were dedicated to their empire. Caze, especially. And she had a planet on the brink of destruction and a sister lost in space.

The last thing Lara needed was a man to complicate things. She shoved a hand through her wet hair. But touching him had been *so* good. Him in her mouth. Watching him let go and enjoy the pleasure. She shivered.

Forcing herself to move, she quickly pressed the controls Caze had used earlier. The tub slid away and the shower stall reappeared. She needed to clean up. She ducked into the shower, turning the temperature to cold. And she definitely needed to cool off.

After she was clean, she pulled on the clothes he'd brought for her. The shirt was a gorgeous blue, the fabric silky on her skin. The trousers were a little snug across her ass, but they'd do. Next, she finger combed her hair.

"Lara."

She spun and saw him watching her from the doorway. She felt a spurt of heat inside. He was just so damn handsome and good to look at.

God, you aren't some swoony, teenage girl.

"Eve is on the comm," Caze said.

"What?" Lara hurried out of the bathroom. In the living area, the large screen on the wall was lit up and filled with her sister's face.

"Eve!"

"Lara!"

"My God." So much emotion stormed through Lara. "You made it."

Eve smiled. "I did. I kidnapped the war commander and didn't die. Piece of cake."

Lara laughed.

Then Eve raised a dark brow. "And you stole three sacred Eon gems, *in* Eon space."

Lara winked. "Child's play."

"I'm so glad that you're okay, Lara."

"You, too."

"I'm glad Caze found you."

Lara flicked her gaze to the man in question. He was standing still and straight beside her. "Yeah, he found me. We almost killed each other." In a variety of different ways.

Eve's blue gaze narrowed. "I warned Caze that if he hurt you—"

"He didn't. You know I can give as good as I get, little sis."

Caze made a strangled sound and heat flared in his eyes. Lara knew he was imagining her lips stretched around his cock, not them beating the crap out of each other.

"I didn't trust him, at first," Lara continued. "He was telling me some crazy things."

Eve grinned.

Lara crossed her arms. "Like you being in love. And mated. To an Eon warrior."

"Warrior, get over here." Eve waved a hand.

A huge male stepped into view. Like all Eon warriors, he was tall and muscled, and his black shirt stretched to the limit across a hard chest. He had an aggressively masculine face, one that carried an air of command.

Lara had seen pictures of him before—War Commander Davion Thann-Eon. She watched as he slid an arm across Eve's shoulders, pulling her close to his side.

And the serious look on his face changed. Lara sucked in a breath. Yep, the war commander was in love with her sister. And her tough-as-nails sister returned the look, her face softening.

Well. A strange feeling coiled in Lara's gut. Without intending to, her gaze flicked back to Caze.

He was watching the couple with an unreadable look on his face.

"It is a pleasure to meet you, Lara," Davion said.

"War Commander."

"Please, call me Davion. I wish circumstances were different."

Lara sighed. "Me, too."

"The Eon have agreed to help us against the Kantos," Eve said.

Lara was elated at having that fact confirmed. "And Wren?"

Eve's face fell. "No word, but we're looking."

Damn. Where the hell was their baby sister?

Eve shifted closer to the screen. "Lara, we need the gems returned. We received intel that the Kantos plan to steal them."

Oh, shit. "Uh..."

Davion's face hardened. "What happened?"

Caze stepped closer behind Lara, and she felt his fingers brush the small of her back. A small comfort.

"The Kantos attacked us on Tholla," Caze said.

"We heard ships had been sighted on the moon." Davion's jaw tightened. "It is brazen of them to be so deep in Eon space. And unacceptable."

"They ambushed us in my ship," Caze said.

"*Cren,*" Davion bit out.

"We were taken to one of their cruisers," Lara added. "But we managed to escape."

"Lara was injured," Caze added.

She turned her head and glared at him. Did he *have* to bring that up?

"What?" Eve demanded.

"I'm fine." Lara held up a hand. "We stole a swarm ship and got to this nifty Eon stealth station. Caze healed me." She left out the bits where he licked her until she came on his mouth, and when she sucked him until he spilled all over her. Their gazes met again, and for a second, she knew they were both back in the washroom.

"The gems?" Davion asked.

"We recovered two of them." Caze's tone vibrated with anger. "But they sent one off-ship. The gem of Eschar."

Davion and Eve cursed together.

"So the gems of Ston and Alqin are safe?" Davion asked.

Caze nodded. "Right here with us."

"It is imperative we get the gem of Eschar back, Caze."

Caze nodded. "Is there more to this?"

"Intel has come in that the Kantos *really* want the gems. We just don't know why, yet."

Shit. Not good. Lara tapped her fingers against her thigh.

"Caze, your mission is still active," Davion said. "You are to recover the gem of Eschar. Whatever it takes."

"Yes, War Commander."

"There's no time to return Lara to the *Desteron*. She can stay with you, and you keep her safe until you get the gem."

Lara growled. "I can keep myself safe."

There was a faint flicker of a smile on Davion's face. "You sound just like your sister."

Eve slapped his chest.

"I can help Caze," Lara said. "I feel responsible for this." She met Eve's eyes. "I want this alliance to work as much as you do."

Her sister nodded. "Then find that gem."

"And you find our sister."

CAZE LED Lara into the nerve center of the station.

"Oh, wow." She looked around, taking in the screens and work tables. Many of the video displays had information scrolling on them. There was a look of desire on her face.

The same look she'd given him when she'd touched him in the washroom.

Instant need stormed through Caze. *Cren.* They had a mission. He couldn't think of having her naked beneath him.

He locked the feeling down. But for the first time in his life, it was hard to do.

He sat down in front of a screen. "We have intelligence probes, informants, and stealth agents sending back data on the Kantos and other enemies of the Eon Empire."

Lara sat beside him. She looked far too delectable in her Eon clothes. "Impressive."

Caze connected with his helian, and a cable

branched out from the scales at his wrist. He hooked into the computer.

She was staring at his wrist. "How long have you had your helian?"

"Warriors are bonded with the symbiont at puberty. A few years after we enter the Eon Military Academy."

Her face hardened. "You make children into warriors."

"The training takes years, as does learning to bond and command your symbiont."

She blew out a breath. "Is it true that some don't survive the bonding?"

He inclined his head. "A few are unable to withstand the transition. They are remembered for their sacrifice."

Lara shook her head. "I think kids deserve to be kids, but I can't argue with the abilities the symbiont gives you."

"Bonding with helians is what helped create the Eon Empire. When our first warriors, Ston, Alqin, Eschar, and Cren first bonded with the symbionts, it changed everything." Of course, Cren had betrayed the others.

"Where do the helians come from?"

He raised a brow. "That is a well-kept secret."

"Can't blame a girl for trying."

"I will tell you they come from certain ore mined in a secret location. The organisms survive in the rock, but cannot thrive without a biological host."

"The sacred gems—"

"Contain some of the earliest helians ever found. From the same source where the first warriors originally discovered the creatures. But those helians are very old, and wouldn't survive the transition to a host."

As he started scrolling through data, Lara's fresh scent came to him. She'd washed with the soaps in the washroom and she smelled clean and crisp. But beneath that was the scent he was starting to know so well, since it was buried in his senses—it was all Lara.

And now he knew the taste of her as well.

A taste he was still hungry for. The need felt worse now.

Caze stared at the screen. *Focus on the mission, warrior.* Thankfully, even though his head was filled with Lara, data was flowing on the screen, and his helian was helping him to sort through it.

He saw Lara touch the screen beside him, studying information on the Kantos.

"Can you narrow down the Kantos vessels in the location of the ship we were on?" she asked.

He nodded. "I've located four that could have transported the gem."

"Shit." She tapped her fingers on the table. "Okay, it's a start."

"Two of them met with larger ships. The other two disappeared."

Her shoulders slumped. "So we have no strong leads."

"We keep looking." He forced himself to focus on the information, searching through the data. The minutes slipped by.

Lara helped him, and they worked surprisingly well together. He already knew that they fought well together, but knowing that they could do this quiet, slow job as well surprised him.

She stood. "I'm going to grab us something to eat."

He nodded, and she was back soon with food and drinks. She handed him a mug, and he sniffed the unfamiliar, warm drink.

Cautiously, he sipped it and paused. "What is this?"

"I rigged your synthesizer to make coffee." She lifted her own mug and took a large sip. Then she made a noise like a purr. "Mmm, caffeiney goodness."

Caze sipped the strange drink again. He liked it. His helian detected the caffeine stimulant, but it had a limited effect on his system.

"I added loads of sugar." She smiled at him over her mug. "I think you need a little sweetening up."

He shook his head. No one in his life teased him like she did. His father never had, his trainers at the Academy never had, and certainly never his fellow warriors.

Caze reminded himself that he ate and drank for sustenance, not for enjoyment. He nodded at her. "This tastes fine."

She rolled her eyes, but her knowing smile said that she knew he liked it.

"Try the snacks." She pushed a plate toward him.

He eyed the unfamiliar things warily. He tried a few nibbles, and flavors exploded in his mouth.

"That cheese is brie. And that's my favorite salami." She dipped a cracker into a bowl of green goop. "And this is the best invention known to man, guacamole."

Caze took his time testing all the food. He couldn't help but savor the delicious tastes. And he couldn't stop himself from watching Lara as she ate. The woman moaned and licked her fingers, relishing every little thing.

Then a chime sounded from the computer and he frowned.

"What is it?" She leaned forward.

"A message. An information broker is asking around...about the gem of Eschar."

She straightened. "You think this broker knows something useful?"

"Perhaps."

"Is he Eon?"

"No." Caze looked at her. "He's Kantos."

She went stiff. "What?"

"He's a defector. He lives in the Hyrokkin Quadrant. It's right on the edge of Eon space and is essentially lawless. There are no rules and no law enforcement. Several species have made their home there, so it's a melting pot of aliens."

"Okay," she said slowly.

"We're going to visit this broker. He lives on a planet called Titania."

Lara leaned over and tapped the screen. Then she hissed.

Caze saw the images she'd brought up. It showed Titania, a small world surrounded by layers of space junk.

"The surface isn't much better," he told her. "It's covered in junk, trash, and scrap. It was an old dumping ground for the Oronis."

She tilted her head. "The Oronis? I've never heard of them."

"Another species who are also closely related to the Eon. They are warriors as well, and allies. Since they relinquished Titania, the denizens of Hyrokkin have claimed it, and added to the mess. Most residents are in the scrap business. Stripping old starships and selling the parts and scrap."

Lara stood. "Well, let's get moving. Um, are we taking the swarm ship?"

"No. There are Eon stealth ships in the hangar."

She rubbed her hands together. "Can I fly it?"

"No." He made his way toward the door.

She followed, frowning. "Why not?"

"It's an Eon ship. I'm the Eon warrior, so I fly."

"Just a little turn?"

"No."

Her blue eyes narrowed. "I'll bring you around, warrior."

The promise in her voice had heat arcing between them.

Caze tried to remind himself that they had no time for the fierce attraction between them. The mission came first. "We'll see, Earth warrior."

CHAPTER TEN

They approached Titania and Lara stared in shock, amazed at the space junk everywhere.

The debris looked like a cloud surrounding the small planet. The surface was dark—no visible water or vegetation. Several ships of varying shapes and sizes were landing and taking off.

After the Climate Wars, Earth had finally pulled its collective head out of its ass and learned to manage the planet's environment. On Titania, it appeared the opposite was going on.

She glanced to the side and saw that Caze was focused on flying. He was bringing them in through a docking lane, his hands moving expertly over the controls.

She imagined them on her skin and licked her lips.

Lara wasn't made for relationships, but she would enjoy her hot warrior for as long as she could. When they parted ways, she'd take some sexy memories with her. Strangely, the thought gave her an odd feeling in her gut.

She shook her head. Now wasn't the time for naughty, lustful imaginings.

"Would you like to bring us in?"

Caze's deep voice jolted her out of her thoughts. "Really?"

"I would have offered earlier, but deep-space flying is—"

"Boring."

He shot her a small smile. "And you don't do boring."

God, she liked him. He already knew her pretty darn well.

He waved her over and she slid between his legs. She pressed her butt between his thighs on the edge of his chair and his arms closed around her.

For a second, she breathed him in, all thoughts of flying leaving her head. Then his deep voice started talking in her ear, and she made herself follow his instructions.

He guided her through the docking beacons, and she laughed, dodging hunks of space junk. They moved in under a larger ship.

"You're a natural," he said.

They descended through the planet's atmosphere, and she got a full view of the city below.

Only one word could adequately describe it—ugly.

Haphazardly constructed apartment buildings, large, grimy warehouses, and towering piles of junk stretched as far as she could see. Factories covered in chimneys pumped thick, black smoke into the air. It wasn't pretty at all.

"There's the space port," Caze said.

From what she could see, most of the space port was subterranean. Large, horizontal hangar doors were open, with ships flying in and out.

Caze took over for the landing, maneuvering their ship into line. Soon, they lowered down into the main hangar. The cavernous space was lined with walkways, and ships were lined up everywhere. The majority appeared to be large cargo haulers.

He brought them in to land—smooth and easy—and they parked beside a giant cargo freighter.

Lara rose, checking her weapons and borrowed light armor. The Eon stealth station had been well-stocked and she'd found gear to fit her. Caze did some final checks on the ship before they both strode off.

As they descended the ramp, the sharp smell of things burning hit her nostrils. A small robot hovered in the air before them, dome-shaped and silver, with several green lights flashing on it.

"Welcome to Titania. Your account will be charged the standard docking fee," the synthesized voice droned.

Caze strode straight past it.

They went up a set of metallic steps, their boots echoing. Then they moved onto a wide walkway. They passed several groups of beings, and Lara felt a spurt of excitement. Many of the species were completely new to her. Earth's space travel had exploded over the last few decades, but the Space Corps still mainly stuck to their own solar system.

They passed a giant, open doorway, and she glanced into the vast space. Several people in huge welding masks were working on a rusty ship. She realized they were cutting it up for scrap.

Crossing a covered walkway to another building, she glanced out a grimy window. "All the buildings are linked by walkways?"

He nodded. "The air quality outside isn't very good. Most residents of Titania stay indoors."

Caze led her a short distance and she realized they were in the lobby of one of the grungy apartment buildings. They passed under a panel of glass roof and she looked up. The building rose above, looking like someone had randomly stacked boxes on top of one another without bothering to line them up straight.

He led her into an elevator and touched the controls.

The doors squeaked closed and she winced. "Pretty sure we're risking our lives in this hunk of junk."

The elevator lurched upward, gathering speed. It jerked to a halt hard enough to rattle her bones, and finally the doors opened. The corridor was a bland beige, with worn flooring, and several laser burns scoring the walls. *Nice.*

She followed Caze and he stopped in front of a door marked with alien text she couldn't read. He thumped a fist against it.

A damaged panel beside the door blinked. "The resident is not home."

Caze grunted and Lara raised a brow. Then Caze lifted a boot...and kicked the door down.

A Kantos stood in the entry, staring at them with four beady, yellow eyes.

He looked like every other Kantos soldier she'd ever

seen, although less muscular. His chest was sunken, and he had several piercings in one cheek.

"Uh, warrior, I wasn't expecting you."

She blinked at the deep, robotic voice. That's when she noticed a metallic box implanted into the skin at his neck. Some kind of tech that let him talk aloud.

"I bet," Caze said darkly.

Lara straightened, keeping her gaze on the Kantos. He might be a defector, but her brain couldn't accept that he wasn't the enemy.

Caze took a menacing step forward, and Lara crossed her arms over her chest. She liked watching him be badass. It turned her on.

"I'm here for intel, Degam. On the gem of Eschar."

"Oh. Heard it was stolen from the temple." The Kantos fidgeted nervously.

Lara stepped closer. "Right. It was stolen by me, but then someone else took it. One of your kind."

Degam's yellow eyes blinked and he licked his thin lips. He looked her up and down.

"Tell us what we don't know," she said.

"Wait, you're Terran." The Kantos eyed her eagerly. "I've never seen your species before."

"Degam." Caze loomed over the Kantos. "Intel. Now."

The alien shrugged his shoulders. "I've got nothing—"

Lara slammed into him. With a screech, he scuttled sideways and hit an overlarge, padded stool designed for a being with four legs.

"I don't like Kantos," she said. "So talk, or you'll be giving me a reason to show my displeasure."

"You do his dirty work?" Degam snapped.

"He's capable of doing his own." She leaned in. "I just enjoy it more."

"The Kantos have the gem," Degam said.

"Why?" Lara demanded.

"They want Earth, and they want the vast majority of Eon territory, as well."

Idiots. The Kantos really believed they could take on the Eon?

"Why do they want the gem, Degam?" Caze asked.

"They need it for the weapon they're creating."

Weapon. Lara froze. *Fuck.*

Caze went motionless, just a muscle ticking in his jaw. "What kind of weapon?"

"The big kind. A planet killer."

Lara felt like a starship had landed on her chest. This was beyond bad.

"Where is the gem?" Caze asked.

"I... Well..."

Lara slammed Degam again.

He screeched.

"Go ahead and lie, Degam," she drawled. "See how I like it."

"I don't like your friend, Caze."

Lara rolled her eyes. "Boohoo."

Caze shook his head, clearly amused. "Where is the gem?"

"You don't pay me enough—"

Lara punched Degam in the face.

The Kantos wheezed. "Tyloth. A hive station near Tyloth."

Caze cursed, long and loud. "Let's go, Lara."

She nodded, giving Degam one last, hard stare.

Her arm brushed Caze's as they strode to the door and her skin tingled. Lara shoved the feeling aside. For now. But first chance she got, she was going to ride the warrior hard and get this damn crazy attraction out of her system.

Degam scuttled forward. "My payment—"

"I'm not sure you deserve it, Degam," Caze said.

Caze and Lara strode down the corridor, leaving the Kantos growling and snarling in his dwelling.

"Tyloth?" she asked. "Hive station?"

They re-entered the elevator. "A hive station is where the Kantos breed their bugs and soldiers."

He didn't sound happy about it. "You've seen one?"

"I've been aboard."

"Once was enough, right?"

"Right. But unfortunately, it's been a few more times than that."

They exited the elevator, through the lobby, and then moved back out onto the main concourse. "So we need to get to the station and sneak aboard."

Silver-black eyes flicked her way. "No, *I* need to sneak aboard."

She frowned. "No way, hot stuff. We're a team."

"You'll stay on my ship."

"No."

Caze jerked to a halt. She thought he was stopping to face off with her, but she saw him staring down the concourse. She followed his gaze and saw several more dome-shaped bots floating in front of them. Five in a row.

"Your security clearances have been revoked," the bots said in unison.

She frowned. "I thought you said this place was lawless? If there's no law enforcement, who owns these bots?"

"There are several syndicates that operate on Titania. They run the salvage businesses...and other things. They also protect their interests, and will do anything to squeeze a profit from a situation."

A lightbulb went off. "They want to take us out and salvage your stealth ship."

"I suspect so. Eon tech does go for a very high price."

All the lights on the bots blinked red.

Uh-oh.

"You are now considered hostile targets for neutralization," the bots droned.

"*Cren,*" Caze spat. "Degam sold us out."

The little weasel. Small doors opened on the bots and weapons extended out, swiveling around to aim at Lara and Caze.

Shit, they had no cover.

Caze held up his arm and his helian morphed. It elongated, forming a silver, rectangular shield in front of them.

The security bots fired and the shield absorbed the laser blasts, flickering with each hit.

"Lara, behind me," Caze ordered.

She moved in close to his back and drew her blasters. If he thought she was going to cower behind him like a helpless princess in an old-fashioned fairy tale, he was sorely mistaken.

CAZE KEPT his arm and shield up, his helian taking the brunt of the blasts. But he felt the pressure of the blows and gritted his teeth against the force of it.

Return laser fire whizzed past him. He turned his head and saw Lara had ducked out from behind him. She was firing her blasters in quick succession.

The security bots focused on her location and she ducked back behind him. The bots' fire slammed into where she'd been a split-second ago. Black marks scored the floor.

"Lara!"

She rolled, coming out on the other side of his shield. She fired again and one bot slammed into the wall.

She grinned. "I've got this, hot stuff."

Leaping up, she strode forward, her entire focus on the bots, her blasters clenched in both hands.

"*Cren*, Lara!"

She fired again, ducking the laser blasts that came her way.

Cursing, Caze charged forward. He could watch the woman fight all day long, but he didn't want to see that pretty skin of hers singed by laser burns.

She fired again, and another bot careened to the side and dropped to the floor. Laser fire scored the walls and he lifted his shield, trying to get in front of Lara. He saw her body jerk.

"Lara!"

"Just winged me. I'm fine." Her gaze narrowed. "Bastard." She concentrated fire on the bot that had caught her.

Caze morphed his helian into a blaster. A big one.

Boom.

His shot took out a third bot. Lara smiled at him, then dived gracefully and rolled. She slid in beneath the remaining bots.

Turning onto her back, she aimed up, and fired both the weapons. The bots started smoking and dropped.

Lara rolled to the side and rose to her feet.

"Four to me, one to you, hot stuff. You're slipping."

Caze ignored her teasing and moved over to check her arm.

"It's fine," she said.

Still, he hated seeing her charred flesh. "We need to get back to the ship. Now."

Together, they broke into a jog. But they hadn't gone far when he heard the thunder of running footsteps.

"Hm, I think we have company." She checked her blasters.

They turned a corner and, ahead, Caze spotted several armed guards. They were all wearing exoskeletons—which gave them added strength, stamina, and weapons.

No doubt more goons who worked for one of the salvage syndicates.

Cren. He nudged Lara through a side door.

They stepped into another large, cavernous warehouse. Nearby, welding bots hovered, working on a large starship, cutting it into recyclable pieces.

Oil puddles covered the floor, and the smell of something burning filled the air. Caze ducked under some pipes and waved Lara on.

Running footsteps and shouts sounded behind them.

Caze and Lara bent over, moving beneath the hull of the starship.

"You aren't a boring date, warrior."

He scowled at her. She was making a joke while they were running for their lives?

"That way." She pointed. "We're close to the hangar, right?"

He nodded, and they skirted some welding bots and stacks of salvaged metals. Laser fire winged through the air, leaving scorch marks on the metal hull of the ship.

Caze lunged, knocking Lara out of the way. A laser blast hit his arm. He felt a flash of pain, and then it was gone.

"Keep going," he roared.

They ran to the far wall.

"Door, door." Lara jogged along it. "We need a door."

"Up there." He jerked his head upward, at a mesh walkway overhead. There was a door in the wall on the upper level.

She frowned. "They'll fire on us—"

Caze gripped her waist and boosted her up. She cursed, but gripped the metal framework of the mezzanine and started to climb.

He turned, firing his blaster at the incoming guards. He'd keep them busy so she could get up there safely.

"Come on, Caze," she called down.

He looked up and watched her pull herself over the railing. She crouched, and started firing on the guards to give him cover.

Caze bent his knees and jumped high. He gripped the metal frame and started climbing. He normally completed solo stealth missions, so he wasn't used to having someone watching his back. Even on the *Desteron*, he was used to giving orders to the security team. He wasn't used to having a partner.

He leaped over the railing, just as laser blasts hit close by.

"Move," he ordered.

She rolled her eyes. "I thought we should stay here and hang out. Have a party."

He nudged her away from the railing. "Sarcasm later, Earth woman."

They raced toward the door. They burst through it and into the hangar.

"There." She pointed to their ship. "Shit."

It was surrounded by several security bots and guards in exoskeletons.

Cren.

"Too many for us to take on alone. Plus, they'll have reinforcements on the way." She glanced his way. "Plan?"

No panic or alarm. No, Lara's face was alive, and she was humming with energy. He wondered if anything knocked Lara Traynor off her stride.

He forced himself to study the hangar below. None of their options were particularly good.

Then Lara snapped her fingers. "See the neighboring ship?"

He turned and looked at the larger Deloo freighter.

"We jump onto it," she said. "Then we leap off it onto our ship."

He looked at her, then at the large gap between their ship and the freighter. He'd never met a woman as fearless as her.

"We'll make it." She smiled. "Watch."

She climbed up onto the railing, pressing her boots onto it, one hand gripping it to keep her balance. Then she jumped.

Caze's heart leaped into his throat. He watched her fly across the gap to the Deloo ship. He held his breath. *Cren*. She wasn't going to make it.

She hit the side of the ship, clinging for a second, then she scrambled up on top of it.

He released a breath. *By the warriors*. The woman was going to drive him out of his mind. He climbed onto the railing and jumped.

He landed in a crouch on top of the freighter, right beside her.

Her nose wrinkled. "Show-off."

They swiveled, creeping closer to the other edge of the freighter. The bots and guards hadn't noticed them.

"Ready?" she asked.

He grasped her hand. They stood, took a running leap, and jumped together. They landed on the top of his stealth ship, their boots echoing dully on the metal.

He heard Lara suck in a breath.

Below, a security bot swiveled. Its lights turned red

and an alarm rang out.

Caze saw the guards turn and shout. Laser fire lit up the hangar.

By Ston's sword. He lunged for the top hatch of his ship. He wrenched it open, and Lara jumped inside. He ducked a laser blast and followed her, slamming the hatch closed behind him.

Lara was already at the controls, her hands moving fast. When he reached her, he felt the ship's engines ignite. Then she turned, gripped the neck of his armor and yanked him to her.

She pressed a hard, quick kiss to his lips. "Let's blow this pop stand, warrior."

"Pop what?"

She elbowed him and turned back to the controls, sinking into the chair. "It means let's get out of here."

Caze sat in the pilot's seat, connecting with the ship's controls. Soon, they were blasting out of the space port and soaring into the night sky.

"Two fighters incoming." She tapped her screen.

He meshed with the cameras and saw the incoming fighters. He flicked on stealth mode and turned his ship sharply to the left. The fighters screamed past them, laser fire arcing uselessly through the sky.

"They're turning back," she said.

Caze released a breath. Ever since he'd realized Degam had sold them out, all he'd wanted was to ensure Lara's safety. He thought it best not to mention that to her.

Lara smiled at him. "You are definitely not a boring date, hot stuff."

CHAPTER ELEVEN

"How long to reach the hive station?" Lara asked. "It's a long hop. We need to stop, stock up on weapons, and get our wounds healed." He eyed her. "And get some new armor for you."

Her arm was throbbing, but it wasn't bad. "You know a place?"

"Yes, another stealth station. This is a planetary one, near the border of the Tyloth Quadrant."

She nodded. "Sounds like a plan."

The control console chimed and Caze touched it. "Incoming call. From the *Desteron.*"

A handsome warrior's face appeared on the screen. He looked almost like a clone of Davion, but Lara noted a few differences. This man had interesting lines around his mouth that said he smiled more than the war commander.

"Brack," Caze said.

The man inclined his head, his curious blue-black gaze falling on Lara before moving back to Caze. "Good to see you alive and all in one piece. We got word of an altercation on Titania."

Caze nodded. "A slight...problem with our informant."

"Davion is waiting for an update." Brack's lips quirked. "And you're surviving working with your new...partner?"

Caze made a sound and Lara raised a brow. "The partner is sitting right here. And he's doing fine. I've barely even beaten him up much."

The man on the screen's smile widened. "I look forward to meeting you another time, Lara Traynor. Hold for the war commander."

An Eon logo flashed on the screen.

"Brack?"

"A fellow warrior on the *Desteron*, and often an annoyance. He enjoys..."

"Pressing buttons. Poking. Needling."

"Yes."

Eve's and Davion's faces appeared on the screen.

"You're okay?" Eve asked.

Lara nodded.

Davion's face was serious. "What happened?"

"Degam sold us out," Caze said. "We had to...finesse our way out."

Lara elbowed him. "He means fight our way out and make a huge mess."

Eve laughed, then her gaze moved between Lara and Caze. Lara saw speculation.

Great. Sitting back in her chair, Lara kept her face

clear of emotion. The last thing she needed was her newly-in-love sister digging where she wasn't needed.

"Caze," Davion said. "We have intel that the Kantos are pushing hard to find you. They want the gems."

"That's not going to happen." Caze pulled in a breath. "We got information from Degam on why the Kantos want the gems."

Davion's brow creased. "Tell me."

"They're building a weapon. I assume they need the gems to make it function."

Davion cursed.

"The gem of Eschar is on a hive station in the Tyloth Quadrant."

The war commander cursed again. "Wait for us. We'll meet up with you, and infiltrate the hive station with a team of warriors."

"They could already be testing a weapon, Davion," Caze said. "It'll take too long for you to get here."

"Degam said the weapon is powerful," Lara added. "A potential planet killer. They want to go after Earth, then the Eon homeworlds."

"Fuck," Eve muttered.

"Caze and I will retrieve the gem," Lara said.

Caze's unhappy gaze turned her way.

She held up a hand. "No arguments, warrior. You know I'm capable."

He blew out a breath. "Lara and I will retrieve the gem."

Eve looked worried. "Be careful."

"Careful is my middle name," Lara said.

"No, it's not," Eve replied. "'Blow it up' is your middle name."

Lara smiled and shrugged a shoulder. "We'll be careful."

Davion nodded. "Keep the gems of Ston and Alqin safe, and bring the gem of Eschar home. And stay alive."

Eve lifted a hand and Lara did the same. The call ended.

Afterward, Lara watched Caze slip into a brooding silence. She monitored the screens and kept glancing his way. A muscle was ticking in his jaw.

"We're approaching an asteroid field," she said.

He nodded. "The stealth station is on the other side. Don't worry, the navigation computer can avoid the asteroids."

She swiveled her chair to face him. "You okay?"

"No."

"Do you want to talk about it?"

"No."

Silence fell again.

"Do you want to fight?" she asked.

A faint smile crossed his face. "I'm just angry. Angry that the Kantos have the gem of Eschar. Angry about this weapon and their plans."

"You're just pissed you aren't a superhero, and weren't able to stop this earlier."

He frowned. "Superhero?"

"Someone from stories on Earth with special skills who always saves the day." She slapped his arm. "Sorry to inform you of this, warrior, you're just a man."

"I'm an Eon warrior."

"Right, so one step down from superhero, then."

He shook his head. "Mostly, I'm angry that I have to take you back into danger. Right into the heart of a Kantos hive."

Her pulse leaped. No one worried about her. Oh, her sisters did, but they rarely knew the details of her missions. "You know I can handle myself."

"I know. But that doesn't make me feel any better. I..." his intense gaze met hers "...have this overwhelming need to protect you."

Warmth filled her belly. Dammit, this should piss her off, not make her feel good. Her fingers curled around his bicep. "We'll be together."

He pressed his hand over hers. "Together."

The computer chimed. "Entering asteroid field."

Lara leaned forward. Giant rocks came into view, sweeping across the viewscreen. One had a crazy, irregular shape, and she arched her neck to keep it in view. Several more passed them. Hell, it was a pretty amazing show.

"Hey," she said. "Some of these asteroids are glowing."

"It's pronyx," Caze said. "Some asteroid miners risk their lives to mine the ore."

Their ship slipped beneath another enormous asteroid. There were soft pinging noises, as some small ones struck their shields.

"After the field," Caze began. "We'll—"

Thump.

It was a hard bump from the left side. The ship jolted.

He cursed, his fingers dancing over the console.

She frowned. "I thought you said the navigation program avoided the asteroids?"

"It does. It's never failed."

Thump.

This time the bump came from beneath them. Lara was tossed against her harness, and the ship spun. Alarms started ringing.

Caze's hands moved faster. "Switching to manual control of the ship."

She saw the small cable linking him to the controls pulse. She leaned forward. There were asteroids everywhere.

Thump.

She jolted forward.

"Asteroids are *not* that maneuverable," he bit out. "Anything showing on scanners?"

She searched the screens. "Nothing."

But something was clearly aiming for them. She craned her neck, and this time she spotted…something.

It was just a glimpse of a large shadow. A *huge* shape. Whatever it was, dived beneath an asteroid.

"Shit. There's something out there, Caze."

"A ship?"

"I…I'm not sure. I just got a glimpse of it. It moved like an animal."

There was another hard impact, followed by the crunch of breaking metal. Gasping, Lara tapped the screens. "We've lost part of the exhaust ports."

"Hull integrity breached," the computer said.

Cursing, Caze stared at the controls. "I'm activating auxiliary shielding."

"Hull breach contained," the computer intoned.

"Something is hunting us," Lara said. "Do the Kantos have a bug that can fly in space?"

"Not that I know of. But they're always breeding new monstrosities."

Another bump, followed by something scraping along the side of the ship. Lara's heart was pounding. Suddenly, it seemed quite possible that this thing could tear the ship apart and kill them both.

There was another jolt, and a large tentacle slapped across the viewscreen. Then it was gone, and a large creature sailed past them.

Lara stared at the enormous, yellow eye, and the huge, gaping mouth filled with teeth.

"Oh, fuck."

"We need to use the asteroids for cover." Caze turned their ship, nosing them down. They picked up speed.

"It doesn't show on the scanners," she said, "but you have cameras, right?"

"Yes."

She pulled up the exterior cameras. The screens filled with images and she saw the creature.

"It's coming in from behind us!" Damn, the thing was huge.

Caze jerked the ship to the right. She looked out the viewscreen, then back at the screens. *Where was it?*

Then she spotted movement. *There.* "It's at location 8.16."

He pulled them hard to the left.

"Shit, it's in front of us now!"

She stared at the huge mouth opening in front of them. It was big enough to take a huge bite out of the ship.

Cursing, Caze turned them sharply. But not sharp enough.

Crunch.

The hard impact made Lara's head shake. Alarms blared, and there was a loud hissing sound. She glanced back. Teeth had sunk through the side of the ship.

"Caze!"

"*Cren!*"

"Hull breach." The computer sounded too fucking calm. "Hull breach."

The vacuum from the breach sucked Lara and Caze hard into their chairs. She felt her seat vibrating beneath her.

There was another loud smashing sound, and a tentacle burst through the hull and into the ship.

Then it started spraying poison around. The green fluid hit the floor and walls, burning and sizzling.

THE BLARING alarms grated on Caze's nerves as he fought to seal the breach. It was hard to move against the suction and the stench of poison filled the air.

"Sealing breach," the computer said.

"Activating...weapons," Lara bit out.

He saw an electric blue energy run over the

viewscreen. She'd activated one of the ship's defensive mechanisms.

The ship shook as the creature jerked.

If they were lucky, it might stun the alien. Caze melded with his symbiont. For now, he needed to plug the *Cren*-cursed hole in his ship.

The shields snapped into place. They sliced through the tentacle, and the creature released the ship. He got a glimpse of the monster as it pulled away from the ship. It had several large tentacles along its side.

The tip of the tentacle wriggled around on the floor behind their chairs.

"Ugh." Lara stood and shook her head. "I hate the Kantos." Then she stiffened, looking out the viewscreen. "It's coming back!"

Cren.

Boom.

The monster hit the side of the ship, hard. The other side wall dented inward from the impact. Another tentacle burst through, reaching almost to their chairs. The force of the suction was huge, making it hard to move.

"Hull breach," the computer said again. "Shields are not responding."

Cren. "The tentacle is too far inside." They needed to drive it out in order to seal the breach.

"What the hell do we do?" Lara yelled.

Caze unstrapped his harness. "You fly the ship."

"What? Don't take your harness off—"

As soon as he was free, he was pulled toward the creature. He had to get it out of here, or they'd be dead.

He sailed across the cabin and slammed into the wall, right beside the tentacle. His sword formed on his arm, and he fought to lift his weapon. His muscles strained.

The ship tilted and he slid along the wall, almost rolling into the tentacle.

"Sorry," Lara called out.

Caze lifted his arm and slashed toward the tentacle. But before he could hit it, the tentacle waved around. It slammed into his face and chest.

Agony.

Where the tentacle touched him, he felt the poison burn. He gritted his teeth, trying to think through the pain.

He had to drive off the creature. Had to protect Lara.

"We're free of the asteroid field," she yelled.

Straining, Caze pushed his blade toward the tentacle.

But the strength was draining out of him, the pain increasing. He wanted to scream, but his jaw was locked.

Suddenly, Lara appeared from nowhere, slamming into him.

"*Oof.*" She pressed her hand to his arm, helping him to push.

His sword moved, but there was still a gap between the glowing silver blade and the tentacle.

Lara grunted. "Come on, warrior. Push, or make that sword longer."

He tried to command his helian, but the pain was making it too hard. He shook his head, trying to focus. His vision blurred.

"Longer," Lara said.

Suddenly, his sword lengthened. He felt a burst of strength.

The silver sword sliced through the tentacle, and the creature screeched and pulled back. Lara and Caze were sucked toward the opening.

"Computer, shields!" Lara yelled.

The shield snapped into place, shimmering. The vacuum of the breach cut off, and Caze and Lara fell to the floor. He threw his hands out, landing on his hands and knees. Lara moved, yanking open some of the built-in cabinets.

"Come on, come on." A pause. "Yes."

Holding a cloth, she moved beside him, carefully gripped the tentacle still pressed to his face and chest in the fabric, then threw it off him.

"Computer, full speed to the stealth station," she said. "*Now.*"

The ship's speed increased.

Lara rolled Caze onto his back. He panted through the pain. He felt like the side of his face was on fire.

"God, hot stuff. You made a mess of yourself." Her hand stroked his arm.

She disappeared for a second, then was back with a medical kit. She pressed a wad of cloth to his cheek.

The pain made him groan, his stomach protesting.

"I know, baby." She pressed something against his neck and there was a sharp pinch as she injected him with a stim. "That'll help with the pain." Her face appeared, hovering close to his. "Stay with me." Her gaze drifted down his cheek, pain in her eyes. "God, you're burned to the bone."

"Not so...hot now."

"Sorry, hot stuff, you're so off the scale that even this wound can't knock you down."

"Havv," he croaked.

"I'm on it. Lie still."

He watched through his good eye as she squeezed the red havv onto his cheek. Pain flared and he cried out.

Her hands touched the side of his neck, stroking his skin. "I've got you, warrior."

He'd never let himself trust someone else to take care of his injuries. He always tended his own wounds on a mission. He hated being vulnerable around someone else.

Pale-blue eyes stayed linked with his, and she cupped his uninjured cheek. "It's okay. Relax. I'm here, Caze. I'm not leaving you. I'm not letting anything or anyone get close to you."

"Lara—"

She pressed a kiss to his lips. "I'm right here."

Then Caze passed out.

CHAPTER TWELVE

T hank God for autopilot.

As they approached the small, uninhabitable planet, Lara gazed out the viewscreen. Gray ash and huge, black mountains covered the planet's surface. There was also a dense cover of clouds that filled the sky, letting only weak light from the distant sun filter in.

The place was desolate.

The ship flew in above the clouds, and they made Lara think of a thick, heavy blanket. She looked up, and saw they were heading straight toward an enormous cliff face of black rock rising above the clouds.

She turned and checked on Caze. He was still on the floor and out cold.

But he was healing. His wound was looking better, but the terrible damage to his face and neck made her stomach turn over.

She looked back to the viewscreen. The quicker she got him to the stealth station and safety, the better.

Where was the damn station? She hoped to hell the ship knew where it was going.

"Please confirm identity," the computer said.

Shit. The station needed some sort of code to access it.

"Please confirm identity, or you will be neutralized."

Oh, great. She shoved a hand through her hair. She moved to Caze, crouching beside him. Last time, he'd used his helian to access the station.

"Warrior? Caze?" She stroked his hair. No response.

Swallowing, Lara moved her hand down his scale-armor to his wrist, and gently touched his symbiont. It looked like a sturdy, black leather band. She brushed it and felt a pulse from it.

"Ah, hey, there." She felt silly. "Look, we need to access this stealth station so I can help Caze."

A wave of energy pulsed from the symbiont, washing through her.

Oh. It made her feel a little light-headed. Had that—?

"Approaching the stealth station," the computer said. "Access confirmed."

Yes. "Thanks, super cool helian." She patted Caze's shoulder then jumped back into the pilot's seat. There was a shimmer on the cliff ahead, and Lara gasped.

With the camouflage shielding gone, she could now see the structure built against the rock. It was all glass and metal, with the landing platform jutting out over the huge drop to the valley below.

The stealth ship came in to land—steadily and smoothly.

"Computer, is the air here breathable?"

"Affirmative. While not recommended for extended exposure, the air is not harmful."

Lara quickly yanked out the small, anti-grav stretcher she'd found with the medical kit. She extended it to match the length of Caze's long form and it hovered in the air. She pushed it down and heaved him onto it. She was panting by the time she'd finished. The man was made of hard-packed muscle and weighed a ton. She lifted the stretcher to waist height, then pushed him off the ship.

She walked across the platform toward the large glass doors into the stealth station. She could feel the air was thinner and she had to use more effort to suck in deeper breaths.

The doors opened soundlessly for them.

She walked inside and her chest hitched. The place was kick-ass. The floor-to-ceiling windows showed an unobstructed view of the clouds clogging the valley between two ridges of mountains.

"Welcome to Lentz Station," a modulated computer voice said.

Dragging her gaze off the scenery, she studied the living area. It was spread over several levels and done in cool grays.

It didn't take long to find a bedroom and get Caze settled on a bed. His armor retracted and she checked his wounds.

She blew out a breath. They were looking much better, and she was so glad she couldn't see bone anymore. Some of the tension eased out of her. After giving him another healing stim, she left him to sleep.

Her stomach growled. Next up, find something to eat. Now that she knew he was safe, exhaustion settled on her like a heavy weight. She forced herself to swallow down some food. She knew very well how important it was to relax in between stressful situations. The body and mind needed to recharge to cope with whatever came next.

Like an automaton, she found the washroom, stripped her clothes off, and took a quick shower to wash off the grime. She scrubbed perfunctorily and wrapped herself in a drying cloth.

Staggering back to the bedroom, she checked Caze again. His chest was rising and falling steadily.

Lara collapsed beside him and fell instantly into a deep, dreamless sleep.

When she woke, she blinked, feeling groggy and confused. She stretched out a hand and found the bed empty.

She felt a spurt of panic.

Pushing off the sheets, she realized she was practically naked. Discarding the towel, she searched the closet and found a simple white shirt. It would do. She pulled it on and hurried out to the living area.

Her gaze was drawn straight to the windows. The clouds were gone and she had a perfect, dizzying view of the sharp drop down the gray valley below. Overhead, the sky was a pale orange color.

Then she heard sharp bursts of breath.

She turned a corner and found a bare-chested Caze wearing only soft, gray pants. He was doing one arm push-ups.

He'd obviously showered, as his hair was damp. Her gaze went straight to his face, and she saw that his cheek was healed, although still a little pink.

He'd picked the perfect spot to exercise. He had a jaw-dropping view into the rocky valley below. She could even see a narrow waterfall falling down the dark cliff face.

As she moved closer, his brooding vibe hit her. "Caze?"

He didn't pause in his push-ups.

"You okay?" she asked.

"My injuries are healed." He stood. He was as tense as a board. She saw a faint sheen of perspiration on his skin. "I require a few more hours until I'll be at full capacity and ready for us to leave for the hive station. I also sent a message to the *Desteron* to update them."

He sounded like a damn bot. She tilted her head. "What's wrong?"

"I want to rip the Kantos apart with my bare hands."

A wave of anger hit her. Yep, he was pissed. "Look, we—"

"They could have killed you." He sliced a hand through the air, his tone like a blade.

Her heart did an extra beat. "You were the one who got hurt."

Something flared in his eyes. Something dark, primal, and needy.

She moved closer, pressing one hand to his hard chest. "I'm okay. We're alive and breathing."

He stepped back and dropped down again to the

135

floor. He started doing push-ups on his other arm. She watched the play of sleek, sexy muscles in his back.

She wasn't going to leave him to stew and brood. She felt the overwhelming urge to help her warrior. The man didn't know the first thing about relaxing and recharging.

"How about we spar?" She looked around. "There's enough room."

"There are sparring bots in the gym, if I want to fight."

She shrugged. "Guess you're afraid I'll take you."

He lifted his head. "Never."

She held her arms out. "Prove it."

He rose in one smooth move.

She gave him no chance to prepare. She attacked. Dropping low, she swiped her leg out, tripping him over.

With a curse, he fell, but was already rolling. Lara leaped on him, sliding her legs around his neck.

He gripped her thighs and twisted her off him.

She jumped back and they both circled each other. Then they charged.

She kicked and hit at him, he blocked. They traded blows. She blocked one of his chops with her arm and the blow made her bones rattle.

But it also made her blood fire.

Oh, yeah. She kicked at him again. He grabbed her foot and twisted.

Lara leaped with it, spinning, and kicking out with her other foot. Her heel caught his jaw.

He released her with a grunt.

She danced back and laughed. "Come on, warrior. I'm barely breaking a sweat."

With a growl, he rushed her.

Shit. Lara spun and ran.

She didn't get far. He took her to the ground. She was pressed to the floor on her belly, a big, hard warrior covering her back.

His hot breath puffed against her neck.

"I've never wanted a woman as much as I want you."

His words made her moan. She pushed her ass back against him. She ground against his rock-hard cock.

Then his hands were tearing at her shirt. As he ripped the fabric off her body, she whimpered.

God, she'd never whimpered for anybody. She felt his palm smooth over her bare ass before his hands dipped between her legs, stroking.

He wasn't gentle. And she didn't care. She liked it. She liked him wild and out of control.

His thumb found her clit. His thick fingers plunged inside her.

Lara cried out. Pleasure was a hot, fast rush.

"So tight, Lara. Will my cock even fit here?" Then his fingers were gone.

"No, Caze—"

He yanked her hips up and she felt him shove his trousers down. His thighs brushed against the back of hers and anticipation made her blood boil. His cock brushed against her ass. She pushed back against him.

"Do it, Caze. Take me. Make it feel good for both of us."

He growled. "You'll be sore tomorrow because of me. I'm going to pound my cock inside you and tomorrow, every time you sit or walk, you're going to think of me."

"Yes."

He drove his cock inside her.

Lara screamed. *So good. Too good.*

His hands roughly gripped her hips, then he was driving inside her, grunting with every thrust.

She pushed back against him, giving as good as she got. "Yeah, baby. Harder."

"Take me deep, Lara."

Her throaty moan egged him on and he increased his thrusts, one of his big hands sliding beneath her belly. He thumbed her clit. Her orgasm shimmered on the horizon, and she moaned. It was going to be huge.

Then he pulled out of her and she cried out in protest.

He turned her onto her back.

"I want to watch your face." His voice sounded like gravel.

God. She could barely understand his guttural words. Sweet warmth flooded through her, an unfamiliar sensation. She liked it.

He pressed her legs apart, pushing them up to her chest. Then he slid his thick cock back inside her. He pulled one of her legs in tight to his side. Their gazes locked, and she couldn't look away.

Connected.

Together.

Her orgasm slammed into her, hitting hard. Her fingernails dug into his back. The pleasure stole her breath away.

She arched up. "Caze!"

"My Terran." He plunged a few more times, then groaned as he came inside her. His body was shaking.

"Oh, my God." She flopped back, one hand gripping his arm. Nothing had felt this good. Not ever. "Well, I can report that you are a superhero lover."

That earned her a faint smile. His fingers moved in soothing circles on her thigh. "You're okay?"

"I sure am." She lifted her head and kissed him. "That felt out-of-the-stratosphere amazing."

A smile flirted on his lips. "It did. You make me feel..."

When his words drifted off, she didn't press. "Feel better now?"

His eyebrows winged up. "This was all to break my mood?"

"Yes." She let out a gusty sigh. "The sacrifices I make for a mission."

His fingers brushed her lips. "I heard you cry my name when you climaxed. That had nothing to do with the mission."

"I'm sure you're mistaken."

He rolled onto his back, pulling her so that she straddled him.

"Then I guess we need to try at least once more," he drawled. "See if you scream my name again this time."

She grinned. "You know I can't resist a challenge."

CAZE WATCHED Lara stagger toward the kitchen, wearing a scrap of gray silky fabric she told him was a robe.

"God, my legs feel like wet noodles."

By Eschar, she was so beautiful. Strength, beauty, brains and grit. He couldn't think of a better combination.

He'd never met a woman like Lara Traynor. He'd never had such a tough, uninhibited lover, either.

"Does that mean I win this round?" he drawled.

She looked over her shoulder and wagged a finger at him. "Don't make me come over there and fuck your brains out...again."

Caze smiled. He'd smiled more in the last few days than he had in years. "That's not much of a threat. In fact, just the opposite."

She brought back bottled water and some nutrition packs. They'd made a nest on the floor with blankets and pillows off the couches.

He pulled her down, savoring the feel of her smooth skin. He'd run his hands and tongue over every inch of her. He'd loved every inch of her.

And he'd realized something that she hadn't, yet. She'd controlled his helian on the ship when they were fighting the Kantos space creature. It was Lara who'd lengthened his sword and enabled them to cut the tentacle off the monster, not him.

She'd also told him his helian had granted them access to the stealth station. She'd communicated with it then as well.

Caze was well aware of what that meant.

Lara Traynor was his mate. His heart thudded hard against his chest. His lover, his woman, his perfect match.

The thought should concern him, but it didn't. He wanted her. More than he'd wanted anything.

She jumped on him, pushing him back into the blankets. She pinned his arms to the floor, and straddled his hips. Her body undulated against him and his cock was hard in seconds.

"I'm not going to show you any mercy, warrior."

Caze surged up, need riding him hard. He pinned her beneath him.

"Hey, no fair." She tried to buck him off her.

"If you can't keep me pinned, then it's all fair." He scooped her up, enjoying her gasp.

He carried her to the wall of windows. Then he spun her, pressing her front against the glass. Her gray robe slithered to the floor.

As her naked body touched the cool surface, she hissed. He gripped her hips, caressing her rounded ass. Her palms pressed to the window and a small, husky cry escaped her.

"Tilt this pretty ass for me, Lara."

She did, resting her forehead against the glass. He saw her looking down into the valley below. He shaped her toned cheeks, blood rushing to his cock as it throbbed.

Take. Claim. Mine.

Caze dropped to his knees. "I love eating you, tasting you." He put his mouth on her and she moaned, rocking back against him.

"And you're damn good at it," she moaned.

He licked her again, and then tilted his head to bite

her ass cheek. Hunger pumped through his veins. He was addicted to the taste of her. He took his time, savoring, listening to her curses and begging.

He slid up her body.

"Caze..." A shaky breath. "I was so close."

"Keep that ass out," he ordered.

"Bossy."

Caze freed his cock, rubbing it between her cheeks. Then he nudged forward. He was swollen and hard, and it was so sexy watching his thick cock slide into her hot body.

They both groaned.

He started thrusting hard and fast. Her fingers pressed into the glass. They both looked at a dizzying view as her cries increased. It was only Caze and Lara— her tight warmth and wetness, the pounding of his cock. Their bodies slapping together.

She threw her head back. "Caze."

He felt the ripple of her body on his cock. "Come."

Her head fell back against his shoulder. "Oh, God, Caze—"

"Come on my cock, Lara."

She did, screaming. Her body clamped down on him, impossibly tight. He lost his rhythm, slamming into her.

His release hit him like a blow. He roared her name, his fingers biting into her skin.

Both spent, she slumped against the glass. He stayed, pressed against her, trying to make sure his legs would hold him up.

When he pulled out of her, she made a small, contented sound.

Smiling, Caze pulled her into his arms and carried her back to the blankets. He lay her down and pulled her close to his side.

She let out a sigh. "How long until we have to leave?"

"Soon. We need to make contact with the *Desteron* and prepare for the mission."

Her fingers touched his cheek. He knew she was touching where he'd been injured.

"Promise not to get hurt this time," she murmured.

"If you promise, too."

But they were both warriors. Both military. They knew the risks.

Caze was well aware that his father would be angry and disappointed in him. Disappointed that his son was having sex, wrapped up in a female, and not one hundred percent focused on his mission.

But as Caze breathed deep and pulled in Lara's sexy floral scent, he had no regrets. She was *his*.

After the mission, then he'd work out what this all meant. Convince Lara to take a chance on a military man who knew next to nothing about relationships and women. Find a way to make a woman who didn't believe in love to take a risk.

She pulled him tighter and let out a sigh. "The people of Earth have no clue to the impending danger. They know the Kantos are hostile, but not that they're planning an invasion."

"Your leaders didn't want people to panic."

"Right. I think they deserve the truth." She nuzzled into him. "This weapon scares me. We *have* to stop the Kantos."

"We will. Whatever it takes."

She tilted her face up to his. "We might not make it."

Caze slid a hand into her hair. Whatever happened, he'd ensure she made it. He'd fight for her, kill for her, die for her.

Whatever it took.

CHAPTER THIRTEEN

"Good. You're a natural at flying an Eon ship."

Lara smiled at Caze's words, and finessed the stealth ship's controls. It was a clone of the damaged one the space creature had destroyed.

Eon technology rocked. Caze had let her fly for most of this trip. It had taken her a little while to get the hang of the sensitive controls, but she loved this Eon ship. They'd just crossed the border into the Tyloth Quadrant.

And now they were almost at the hive station.

She looked at Caze. So gorgeous and hot.

The lights from the console threw his handsome face into sharp relief. He was so damn strong. Looking at him, you'd never know how badly injured he'd been just hours ago.

Lara finally acknowledged that she liked him. *Really* liked him. Her fingers clenched. More than she'd ever liked any man before. She, who never let a guy too close, had let this one slip under her radar.

She thought of her mom. Mika had started out tough,

been a damn fine Space Corps lieutenant. But love, and losing it, had wrecked her. Had made her weak.

Lara had vowed that would never happen to her.

She let out a breath. She wasn't her mother. Eve had told her that so many times before.

"The hive station is in visual range," Caze said.

Lara looked at the viewscreen and zoomed in.

Her heart thumped against her ribs. The station looked like an upside-down iceberg floating in space. The conical structure had a large, flat top, and narrowed down to a point at the bottom. It had a dark, rough outer shell, and small ships were flying in and out of the top of it.

"You're sure our stealth will hold?" she asked. "We can get in undetected?"

"Yes. I've snuck onto hive stations before. The last time was for a rescue mission to retrieve a kidnapped warrior. The Kantos never detected my ship."

"Did you get him out?"

There was a pause. "We returned his body to his family."

Her stomach tightened. "I'm sorry, Caze."

He nodded. "I'm going to enjoy sneaking the gem of Eschar out from under them."

Lara smiled briefly. "Me, too."

They flew closer, avoiding the swarm ships. Then Caze directed her to the lower end of the station.

"We'll attach to the outer wall and cut our way in."

Caze took over control, gently finessing their small ship close to the station. *Clunk.*

"Ship attached," the computer said.

He powered down and glanced at her. "Ready?"

She nodded. She ran a hand down the armor she'd selected back at the stealth station. It wasn't as fancy as his helian scales, but it was still very-well-made Eon armor. Then she checked her weapons.

Oh, yeah. She was ready to make the Kantos regret the day they'd targeted Earth. "Bring it."

He stopped at a cabinet and pressed his palm to a lock panel. There was a hiss, and a reinforced drawer opened.

The gem of Ston and the gem of Alqin sat on a bed of shiny silver fabric.

Caze pulled out a small, black pack. He carefully stowed the gems inside. Then he held the bag out to her. "I want you to take care of these. I can't risk leaving them unattended on the ship."

She swallowed. "You should—"

"I'll be the main target of any Kantos we encounter." He paused. "There are very few people I would trust with these."

Chest tight, she took the pack and let him help her slide it onto her back. He tightened it, so it was flush against her spine.

Then, Caze opened a side hatch, and Lara stared at the rough, brown hull of the Kantos station on the other side of the opening.

"How are we getting in?" she asked.

He pressed his palm to the hull, and his hand began to glow silver. Wow, his helian was doing something.

She watched a circular hole begin to form, the edges glowing brightly. The hull slowly melted outward, until a large enough hole formed for them to duck through. A faint, silver shimmer covered the opening. Some sort of force field, it seemed.

Caze went first, ducking through the shimmer. A second later, he waved her in. Lara stepped onto the hive station.

It reminded her of the Kantos ship they'd been held on. The dark walls were rough, with a hexagonal pattern. The lighting was low, leaving lots of shadows.

The inside of the station was filled with an incessant, buzzing hum. From somewhere, she heard a wild scream. It set her teeth on edge.

Caze touched the edge of the hole they used and she watched as the hole began to close. The brown wall grew back again.

"Holy cow." She really, really wanted a symbiont.

Once the hole was closed, Caze looked at the screen attached to his wrist. "Our intel suggests that the main hive station labs are two levels up. That's likely where they've taken the gem."

He moved through an arched doorway out onto a walkway. Lara followed and sucked in a breath.

The central core of the station was empty. It reminded her of the hangar back on the Kantos cruiser, except hundreds of times larger.

Walkways ringed the large space, and in places, cocoons were attached to the walls. Bugs were flying in the center of the open space, their wings fluttering.

Holy hell.

The sound of marching feet caught their ears.

Caze gripped her arm and pulled her back. They slid into a shadowed alcove.

A group of Kantos soldiers marched past them. These ones were young—thinner bodies, their four legs less sturdy, with paler skin. They weren't fully mature yet.

Lara turned her head and realized that she was pressed close to a cocoon on the wall. She saw something move inside and grimaced. No doubt some nasty bug.

"Let's go," Caze whispered.

She followed him out of the alcove. They reached the end of the walkway and moved up a spiral ramp.

The next level looked the same as the one below. It would be so easy to get lost in this place.

He led her through an arched doorway and gunk dripped off the ceiling. It hit her shoulder and she swiftly swiped it off. Her nose wrinkled. It was sticky and smelled bad.

Caze had stopped and she lifted her head. She hissed.

The room was filled with large, circular white eggs. They had a rough surface and came up to about her waist.

A shadow moved inside one.

"What the hell are these?" she asked.

"Pretty sure we don't want to know." He carefully weaved his way through them.

Then they both heard familiar clicking sounds. They turned back to the doorway. Soldiers were coming.

Shit. Caze grabbed her arm and dragged her down. They crouched behind an egg.

She heard noises and peered around the side of the egg. Several soldiers had entered and they were checking the eggs.

She realized they were scientists of some kind.

Lara and Caze waited, her pulse a loud drum in her head. She willed the Kantos to not come in the direction of their hiding place. *Move away. Move away.*

Finally, they flowed out the door.

"We should follow them," she whispered.

Caze nodded. Together, they ducked out from behind the egg and followed the scientists out of the room. In the corridor, they waited a beat. She heard clicking from down the hall.

Hugging the wall, they rounded a gentle curve in the corridor.

Suddenly, a soldier came through a doorway and spotted them. His four eyes widened.

Without speaking, Caze and Lara pounced.

Caze's sword flashed, cutting through the Kantos' gut. Lara leaped high, yanking her knife out. She jammed the blade into the soldier's throat.

His arms flailed, and Caze drove his sword deeper. The Kantos sagged.

Lara straightened. "You think he got a message off?"

"No clue."

Together, they dragged the dead Kantos' body back into the room and behind an egg.

"Let's get this done," Caze said.

They moved back into the hall and toward the next room. At the doorway, they stood with their backs against the wall and peered in.

The lighting was brighter and it was filled with benches. Definitely a lab.

And thankfully, it was empty. They moved through it

quickly. She lifted vats and containers of unidentifiable liquids.

No gem.

Caze jerked his head to move to the next lab.

It was almost identical to the first, except at the back were large, clear vats taller than Lara. They were filled with tiny, writhing larvae.

They looked like maggots and they were feeding on... some sort of animal carcass. "I think I vomited in my mouth a little."

"Searching, Lara."

Right. She moved down the lab benches. Nothing.

They moved to the next lab and there was also no gem.

Caze scowled, lost in thought.

"Any other place on the station where they might take the gem and build a weapon?" she asked.

His scowl deepened. "Their weapons area."

She winced. "Let me guess. It's not close by."

"Another few levels up. Not too far away."

But the longer they stayed on the station, the greater the risks.

She straightened her shoulders. "Let's do this, warrior."

CAZE PULLED himself over the ledge, air sawing in and out of his lungs.

"One. More. Level," Lara gasped from beside him.

They'd climbed up several levels. It had been hard

work, especially when they'd been forced to dodge any Kantos in range.

He watched Lara press her hands to her knees, sucking in air.

She'd kept up with him. She was as resilient and determined as any Eon warrior he'd fought beside.

"There's a ramp over there," he said. "The next level is the Kantos weapons area."

Relief flashed in her eyes. "Good. I wasn't looking forward to more climbing."

Once they'd caught their breath, they jogged to the ramp. Here, the walls were striated and above, he saw pipes and conduits that looked like they were made from organic materials.

They reached the top of the ramp and he pointed to the arched doorway closest to them.

They crossed the corridor and paused, looking inside the room. It was long and narrow, and empty. Caze frowned. The far wall was shrouded in a mist that wafted around like a cloud.

"What the hell?" Lara murmured.

She moved closer, and muttering a curse, he followed. Maybe the gem was hidden behind the mist.

The fog shifted and that's when he saw what it was covering. *Cren.* There was another part of the room and inside were rows of tables.

And on the tables were dead bodies.

He felt his muscles lock. There were lots of different species on the tables. He saw an Eon warrior and he ground his teeth together. He saw others, including an Oronis warrior.

Beside him, Lara gasped. "Oh my God. That man is human."

Caze followed her gaze and saw the shorter human male, laid out and cut open.

She pressed a fist to her mouth. "God."

"We can't stay," he said. "They're dead. We can't help them now."

"We can't *leave* them." Fury vibrated in her voice.

"This isn't our mission." He hated the thought of leaving them. Of leaving a fellow warrior here, his body desecrated.

But right now, they had no choice. And keeping Lara alive and finding the gem were far more important than recovering dead bodies. These people had no need of rescue. They were at peace.

Finally, she gave a small nod, but her face was etched with sorrow.

He nudged her forward and together they moved to the next room. When he saw the interior, he knew they were definitely in the right place. Weapons were loaded on racks attached to the walls and vats of poison were stacked high. Large Kantos missiles rested on stands in the center of the room.

"Jesus." Lara took a stumbling step forward.

"Lara." He gripped her shoulder.

"Look at this weaponry." Her voice was hollow. "They could wipe us out. Obliterate us."

"I'm not going to let that happen."

It was the truth. Less than a week ago, Caze hadn't cared one bit about Terrans or Earth. All he knew about them was that they were chaotic and disordered. The old

Eon king had banned the Eon Empire from having anything to do with Earth.

Now his only exposure was to Eve and Lara—and that was enough for him to make his own judgment. He'd met two interesting, fascinating women, who were both far more than he'd expected. One of those women he was getting to know better than he knew anybody else. Earth was clearly full of billions of unique, flawed, but fascinating humans. None of them deserved to die. And no one deserved to be the prey of the Kantos.

"Let's see if we can find the gem of Eschar," he said.

She nodded, and he watched as she pulled herself together. They quickly moved through the missile room, but there was no sign of the jewel.

Cren. Where was it?

He nodded to the next doorway. He saw yet another strange, empty room. He frowned, staring at the circular designs embedded in the floor. The large, amber-colored circles were the only thing notable about the space.

"Let's keep moving."

They started out across the room.

But Caze hadn't gotten far when his boot landed on one of the circles. He heard a click.

He looked down and frowned.

"Caze?"

The circle beneath his boots dropped away and he fell.

The next second, he was submerged in an amber, gel-like fluid. He kicked his legs, trying not to breathe in the gunk. But it was thick, making his movements difficult.

He reached up, and that's when his palms smacked

into the cover over his head. The hole he'd fallen through was gone, covered over again. He banged his fist against the circular covering.

Splash.

He spun around, kicking to keep himself up. Lara landed in the fluid beside him. She kicked, moving close beside him.

Cren. He slammed his fist against the cover above his head. She joined him, and together, they pummeled the flooring panel.

But it wasn't budging.

He looked at her and saw her eyes were wide. Thanks to his helian and lungs that were several times larger than hers, he could hold his breath for a long time. But Lara couldn't.

He grabbed her hand and kicked, fighting his way through the thick, amber fluid.

They needed to find a way out.

Kicking hard, he searched for any sign of an exit. Soon, they reached the wall on the far side of the room. A blank wall.

Come on. His blood was pounding. He glanced at Lara. She was still holding her breath.

Caze's helian could form a helmet for him once his air ran out, but he couldn't do the same for Lara. He *wasn't* going to let her die.

She pointed.

Farther along the wall, he saw the outline of a door. They swam over and thumped against it. He kicked his boots against the metal, but it didn't move.

He saw that Lara was getting sluggish, her movements uncoordinated.

Cren. He yanked her close, pressing his mouth to hers. He breathed through her lips and she sucked in air from him.

But he heard the countdown in his head. They were running out of time.

No. He was saving this woman. He wouldn't let her die.

He held up his arm, aiming at the floor above their heads. He couldn't form a blaster weapon because the laser fire would rebound in this gel and kill them.

What could he do? How could he get them out?

Suddenly, his helian took matters into hand. A large, solid battering ram formed on his arm.

He smiled grimly. It would do. He held it above his head and kicked. He aimed at one of the circular covers, moving as fast as he could.

Boom.

The battering ram hit the floor above. Nothing happened.

He pulled back, and kicked hard. *Boom.*

Just below him, he saw Lara struggling. She was fighting not to take a breath.

They were out of time.

Fueled by desperation, he kicked again.

Boom.

The floor panel above his head shattered.

Reaching down, his battering ram dissolving away, he grabbed Lara's hand. He yanked her up, kicking his feet with everything he had.

Caze's head burst above the surface of the fluid. He yanked Lara up beside him.

He heard her heave in a breath, then he pulled them both out of the liquid. They collapsed on the floor.

He fell back, sucking in air. Lara fell onto her hands and knees beside him.

"God. God." She pushed her sodden hair off her face.

They were both covered in the sticky fluid.

She held up an arm, droplets plopping onto the floor. "Ugh, this is beyond gross. Have I told you how much I hate the Kantos?"

He reached for her, pulling her close, and pressed his forehead to hers.

He felt a pulse from his symbiont. The warm energy washed over them, drying the amber goo instantly. It fell away like dust.

Lara looked down, her mouth dropping open. Then she shook her hair, the crusty amber flakes falling to the floor.

"Thanks, warrior." She smiled. "For saving me and for the de-gooing."

He opened his mouth to respond, but he heard clicking echoing from the hall outside. They both tensed.

He hadn't exactly been quiet when they'd broken out of the amber fluid. The Kantos were coming.

Lara bounded to her feet. "Time to go."

Caze scanned around. They needed somewhere to hide. The walls were bumpy and rough. Up near the ceiling, he spotted a narrow ledge.

He moved, scooping Lara up into his arms.

She slid her arm across his shoulders. "What are

you—?"

He bent his legs and jumped. They sailed up and Lara gasped, clinging to him. His boots hit the ledge and he crouched down.

"I just have to say this," she whispered. "That was amazing. And a hell of a massive turn on."

He fought a smile. *By Alqin's axe*, she could cause a surge of desire at the most inappropriate times. He pressed a finger to her lips.

Below, Kantos soldiers surged into the room. They rushed over to the broken floor, circling around it. Their clicking increased in volume.

The soldiers stayed a long time, studying the floor and searching the room. He wasn't sure what they'd deduced, but after endless minutes, they finally left.

Caze waited, Lara crouched beside him. No more soldiers arrived. He nodded at her and leaped off the ledge. He was careful to avoid the *Cren*-cursed amber circles. As he hit the floor, he bent his knees.

He spun and held up his arms.

Lara didn't hesitate. She jumped and he caught her.

"How about we leave this room behind?" she suggested.

"I am in total agreement."

He set her down and they weaved between the amber circles. At the next doorway, Caze heard more clicking ahead.

With Lara pressed up beside him, they both peered through the door. His pulse spiked.

In the center of the room, resting on a stand surrounded by Kantos scientists, was the gem of Eschar.

CHAPTER FOURTEEN

There it was.

Caze assessed the situation. They couldn't take on all the scientists without one of them getting a warning off.

Lara held up a hand. She was holding a small device.

"Sedative grenade," she murmured. "Designed for Kantos."

"Where did you—?"

"Last resort device. All space marines have one in the heel of their boot." With a wink, she tossed it into the lab.

It rolled across the floor, and one scientist raised his head, looking around for the noise. Then there was the hiss of gas and a cloud of smoke filled the air.

The clicking sounds went wild, and then Caze heard the thump of a large body hitting the floor. It was followed by several more.

He smiled at his woman. "You are magnificent."

She gave a small bow. "Glad you noticed."

ANNA HACKETT

Together, they moved into the room, stepping over the bodies of the unconscious Kantos.

They reached the gem and Caze lifted it off the stand.

"Thank the warriors." He placed it securely in a small bag attached to his belt. "Let's get out of here."

They turned...just as a huge bug skittered through the doorway.

It had a long, flat body, serrated legs, and long antennae.

"Damn, it looks like a mutant cockroach," Lara said.

The bug screeched and rushed at them.

Lara reached over her shoulder and pulled out her sword. She ducked a leg that came swinging her way.

Caze leaped, his sword held over his head. He slashed down, cutting off the creature's antennae.

Lara slid along the floor, right beneath the creature. She sliced at the creature's belly.

Cren, she was too fearless. He watched as she sliced off one pincer.

The creature reared up. His heart lodged in his throat. She was too close. The *cren*-cursed bug was going to crush her.

"Lara!" He jumped, landing on the bug's side. He rammed his sword into the bug, working the blade through the hard shell.

The Kantos screeched—wild and high-pitched. He saw Lara roll away.

The creature spun and Caze flew off, smashing into a bench. The air rushed out of him.

Lara leaped onto a neighboring bench and jumped

160

into the air. She threw something—a grenade—into the bug's mouth.

It closed its mouth and made a coughing sound. Then there was a muffled thump, and the Kantos' stomach burst open.

Lara landed and rolled. Bits of bug flew everywhere. "Ugh."

Caze brushed a lump off his armor and shook his head. "Back to the ship. Now. We're getting out of here."

She nodded, and together they ran for the door. They burst into the corridor.

A squad of Kantos soldiers was waiting for them. They skidded to a halt.

"Um, ideas, warrior?"

"I'm thinking."

An elite stepped forward. *You have trespassed.*

"We're just taking back what you stole, asshole," Lara snapped.

The elite ignored her, his gaze on Caze.

We have treaties.

"Which you ignored when you attacked our war commander and stole our sacred gems."

The Terrans—

"Are none of your business. The Eon Empire now has alliances with Earth."

An angry clicking echoed off the walls.

Kill them. Take all the gems.

LARA SWUNG HER SWORD, hitting it against a Kantos soldier's arm. She heaved, knocking him back. Then she spun, ducked low, and cut at the legs of another.

Nearby, Caze fought like a tornado. He was spinning, ducking, and slashing. The ground was littered with Kantos body parts and with injured soldiers.

But there were so many. *Too many.*

And more were running up the ramp to get to them.

The Kantos always used their numbers to swarm in and win. With a growl, Lara threw herself into the fight. Energy stormed through her veins.

She'd keep fighting. It was what she did best. She didn't have it in her to give up—not like her mother.

She shot another glance at Caze. Hell, she could spend hours watching the man fight.

A Kantos arm slammed against her gut. Her armor took the brunt of the blow, but the wind was knocked out of her. She gasped, fighting through the pain.

Another swing of a sharpened arm and Lara dropped and rolled. She felt the arm graze her back... And cut through the strap of her backpack.

"No!"

It spilled open, and the blue-green gem of Ston rolled out.

The next few seconds happened in slow motion. Going on instinct, she reached into the torn pack on her back, her hand closing on the gem of Alqin. Without looking at it, she shoved it into the small pouch attached to her belt. Her gaze never left the gem of Ston as it rolled across the floor. The clicking sounds around them went wild. On her hands and knees, she chased after the jewel.

"Lara!" Caze bellowed.

Her hand closed on the stone and she rose.

Right at the very edge of the walkway. There was no railing, and several bugs were flying in the central core, their translucent wings fluttering.

A soldier rushed at her and swung out his arm. Lara ducked.

Shit. One of her boots slid an inch over the edge. She had nowhere to go. Except down, and that wasn't an option.

Another swing of that sharpened arm and she saw the beady eyes focused on the gem. Lara's boot slipped completely off the edge.

She pitched backward into the central core.

Fucking hell.

She shoved the gem of Ston in her belt beside the other one, air rushing past her. She dropped past a flying bug, and she stared up at the hive above her.

Caze. Regret hit her. She wished...

She didn't finish the thought. Instead, she watched in horror as the warrior dived off the walkway above.

Her heart lodged in her throat. *The idiot.* They'd both die, smashed into a million pieces below.

Tears pricked her eyes. Except for Eve, no one had ever risked themselves for Lara. She wanted him to live, dammit, even if a part of her loved that he was coming for her.

His big body slammed into hers, his arms wrapping around her. She clamped her legs around his waist.

"You're a fool!" she shouted.

He lifted his arm and she saw a flash of his helian. Silver shot out from his wrist.

What was he doing? Suddenly, they were jerked to a vicious halt, both of them hanging upright in the air over the central core.

Lara looked up. His helian had formed a silver rope, and it was tied around a flying bug. Its wings flapped madly and it bobbed unsteadily.

It flew across the core, and Lara and Caze spun and jerked beneath it.

"You're crazy," she yelled.

"I wasn't going to let you die, *shara*. Ever."

Lara melted inside but she scowled at him. Lara Traynor *never* melted.

She heard shouts from the other side of the core. The Kantos soldiers hadn't forgotten them. But she ignored them as the bug moved in a jerky zigzag, approaching the other side of the core.

Just a bit closer.

All of a sudden, Caze retracted his helian rope.

Oh God. They fell, and he launched them toward the edge. She held on tight, and then they hit the walkway, skidding across the floor.

They came to a stop, Caze cradling her tight.

Holy hell. They'd made it!

She spun and kissed him.

He pulled back, running his gloved hand along her jaw. He smiled at her. "Save that for later."

"It's a deal, hot stuff. You've earned yourself whatever you want." She leaned in, voice lowering. "Hot and sweet, or wild and dirty. However you want it."

There was a bright flare in his eyes. "That's a very good incentive to get out of here."

HEART STILL HAMMERING in his chest, Caze moved along the walkway with Lara's hand firmly in his.

In his head, he kept seeing her fall. He clamped down on the memory. They had to focus on getting out. *Alive.*

It wouldn't take the soldiers on the other side of the core long to reach them.

Nearby, a bug skittered out of a side tunnel.

Lara shuddered. "I *hate* the spider ones."

That didn't stop her from leaping on the creature, her sword slashing.

The bug screeched and green blood sprayed across the floor. Caze didn't even have time to lift his sword.

Then he heard the dreaded clicking in the air and the hammering of Kantos feet.

Cren. He looked around for a way out. "Lara, in there."

She leaped off the dead bug carcass. They both raced for the doorway he'd spotted. Inside, they turned and pressed against the wall.

The room was filled with eggs. These ones were conical-shaped and brown, with rough shells.

Then Caze heard soldiers outside. *Cren*, he and Lara were about to be discovered.

Several soldiers reached the doorway of the room, but didn't enter.

Caze frowned, listening to their clicking. They sounded agitated. Then, strangely, they retreated.

"We finally caught a break," Lara murmured.

Lifting his wrist, he studied his screen. He only had partial intel on the hive's layout, but he saw what he needed. On the far side of the room there was a vertical tunnel they could use to get back to their ship.

"Over there." He jerked his head. "There's some sort of maintenance access. We can use it to get to the hangar level."

Lara looked across the space and nodded. They started weaving their way through the eggs.

These eggs were larger than the ones they'd seen earlier. They heard more noises from the walkway outside and they froze, lifting their weapons.

But no one rushed in to confront them.

"Why aren't they attacking us?" she murmured.

"I don't know, but let's not waste this bit of luck."

Nodding, she turned, her hip accidentally hitting an egg.

She cursed, touching the sticky residue that clung to her. Her nose wrinkled and she stepped back, trying to shake off the orange substance. It stretched out between her and the egg.

"Lara, move it," he said.

Suddenly, the top of the egg unfurled.

They both froze, watching it. It looked like a flower blooming.

"Uh-oh." Lara stepped back.

A second egg opened, then another. Caze's gut cramped. He didn't like this at all. He grabbed Lara's arm. What ugly, deadly creature was about to emerge?

A flood of small, black insects spilled out of the egg like a wave. They flowed onto the floor.

"What the hell?" She jumped back.

"Get back!" he yelled.

The bugs moved fast. Swarms of the tiny creatures spilled out of the eggs.

Then, there was a wild, angry screech and Caze tensed. A bug scuttled into the room, yellow eyes on them. He could see hunger pulsing in its gaze.

It leaped, landing hard and knocking over an egg. The egg burst, and more black insects spilled out.

They joined with the other swarm and immediately engulfed the bug.

It screeched and thrashed, completely covered in black.

Caze pulled Lara back, keeping her close. They watched, horrified and rapt, as the bug was swamped by the swarm of writhing black.

Then the insects flowed off the bug, leaving only hard shell behind.

All the bug's fleshy parts were gone.

"Fuck," Lara said.

He pushed her. "Run."

They turned, sprinting for the door. They'd take their chances with the soldiers.

As they leaped over the eggs, more of them opened. The growing swarm rushed at them like a giant wave.

They weren't going to make it. The door was still too far away.

More eggs opened, between them and the door. More terrible blackness flowed out.

Cren.

He looked around. He had to get Lara out of there.

But there was no clear path. Then he spotted several large light fixtures dangling from the ceiling.

"Lara." He gripped her waist and jerked his head upward. She nodded, and he tossed her into the air.

She grabbed one light, holding on tight as it wobbled.

Caze moved, feeling the wave of black insects nipping at his boots.

"Caze, hurry!"

He jumped onto an unopened egg and leaped up. He grabbed the light fixture next to Lara's, sending it swinging wildly.

Cren. He hoped the thing would hold.

The swinging slowed, and his gaze met Lara's. She shot him a forced smile. They were okay. For now.

He looked down and his gut hardened.

The entire floor was covered in a heaving mass of flesh-eating insects.

CHAPTER FIFTEEN

Well, shit.

Bugs covered the floor, heaving and surging.

Lara gripped the light fixture tightly, her knuckles turning white. She and Caze hung in the middle of the room, and she was excruciatingly aware that they needed to get moving, or every bug and soldier in the hive would be on them in minutes.

"Ah, Caze—"

"Shh."

So bossy. She looked over at him. His brow was scrunched in concentration. He lowered one arm, hanging from the other one. His symbiont shifted, morphing into some sort of weapon.

She frowned. What was he—?

Flames spewed out from his arm.

Holy hell. She grinned. Her man had made a fucking *flamethrower*.

He sprayed the fire down on the floor beneath them,

and she watched insects below shrivel. He cleared a patch under them.

"Go," he roared.

Lara dropped, landing in a crouch. The burnt husks of the dead bugs crunched under her boots.

She spun around and looked for the door to the tunnel. Caze dropped down beside her, still spraying flames. She felt live bugs brush against her boots and she leaped back.

Caze shifted closer, forcing the wave of insects back with the flamethrower. He carved a path through them.

"Keep moving."

She walked through the narrow gap. There was only a thin strip of insects between them and the tunnel door. She took a running leap and jumped over them.

Behind her, Caze turned in a circle, taking out more bugs and several unopened eggs. The sharp stench of burning insectoid flesh filled the air.

Then she saw an egg open right behind him.

"Caze, watch out!"

Her shout made him turn...just as a wave of bugs leaped on him from the egg.

Her stomach dropped away. *No. Come on, Caze.*

He sprayed more flames, smacking the bugs that were climbing up his arm. They were eating through his armor in patches.

"Get into the tunnel," he yelled.

"Quit playing around and get over here."

He yanked out the gem of Eschar and tossed it at her. She caught the red jewel.

"Go." His voice was unbending. "Get to the ship."

. . .

HE WENT DOWN on one knee under the onslaught.

Screw this. Lara shoved the gem into the pouch on her belt with the others and leaped back over the bugs, with no plan except to help Caze.

Landing beside him, she kicked at the mass of bugs and slapped at the ones on his chest. Some of them clung to her and she felt nips on her skin.

"You are exasperating," he growled.

"You don't get to be a martyr today, hot stuff."

She smacked at the insects again. She could see blood on Caze where they'd eaten through his armor.

She needed her own damn flamethrower.

Suddenly, the scales on Caze's arm shifted. They flowed across the air toward her.

She sucked in a breath. The black scales moved up her skin, covering her right arm. She stared, watching as a flamethrower formed. It glinted silver in the light.

Rock on. She started spewing flames at the insects. *Oh, yeah.* The bugs backed off, and a second later, Caze rose.

His face was unreadable. His gaze went to her flamethrower and he shook his head, as though to clear it. "Let's go."

Her weapon dissolved, and the black scales flowed back into his armor. For a second, Lara felt bereft. Then Caze grabbed her hand and they ran for the door.

He pushed it open, then slammed it closed behind them. They were pressed together in the narrow space.

"Hope those damn things can't squeeze under the door," she muttered.

He crouched and yanked a cover off the floor.

Beneath it was the tunnel.

"Let's not stick around to find out," he said.

Lara started climbing downward. Caze closed the hatch above them and followed her. Their boots rung dully on the metal. "That was wild, by the way." Adrenaline was still charging through her. "How you shared your helian with me."

There was a beat of silence. "I didn't."

"What?" She looked up at him.

"Eon warriors can't share their helian. I've only heard of it happening once."

Lara felt a rush of confusion. "When?"

"With Davion and Eve."

Lara blinked. What the hell did that mean? "Wait..."

"Later, Lara. For now, let's get out of here."

Her mind whirred, but they kept climbing. *Focus, Lara. You can find some time to freak out later.* Soon, the tunnel ended in a quiet, dark room.

"We're close to the ship," he murmured.

She nodded, following him across the dark space. There was an arched doorway across the room, and light shining from outside it. *Almost there.*

Something made a noise in the darkness. A scrape of something large.

A cold shiver went down her spine. She turned her head, searching the shadows.

She couldn't see anything. She picked up speed.

Another movement. Her chest hitched. Then she felt something slither around her waist, like a rope.

What the hell?

She was yanked backward and lifted off her feet.

CAZE HEARD Lara's shocked cry. He spun.

A huge, spider-like bug had her between its two front legs. It was spinning a white web around her legs.

She struggled, trying to hit the creature.

Cren, the thing was big. The same size as his ship.

Caze's sword morphed on his arm. He felt a throb of pain from his helian. The insects had injured him, and his symbiont was working to heal the wounds.

He strode forward. Smaller spiders skittered out of the darkness. They were about waist-high, with furry, black-and-white bodies.

His lips firmed. *Come on, then.*

The spiders leaped at him. He swung his sword, cutting one down, then hacking into the legs of another. He ducked a third creature, and came up to see a fourth spider spraying webbing at him. The sticky substance stuck to his legs. He moved his arm, slicing through the web.

Another spider darted back at him and he jumped over it. He rammed his sword down, skewering the spider from the top.

He landed and looked up.

The giant spider was still spinning its web around Lara. She was covered in white web up to her waist. "I fucking hate spiders." She punched the leg of the creature, but it didn't react.

"I'm coming, *shara*."

She was wrenching her shoulders from side to side, and that's when he saw her pull something off her belt.

She tossed it, and it skidded across the floor toward him.

Grimly, Caze kept fighting the smaller spiders. He went down on one knee, slicing out with his sword in a wide arc, cutting down two more of the arachnids.

"Caze, get the gems and get out," she yelled.

He gritted his teeth and impaled another spider. He ripped his sword back. "You really think I'd leave you?"

"We have a mission."

The web was covering her to chest height now. She was still wriggling, fighting to get free, but she was stuck.

Caze sliced open another small spider. There were more, but they skittered back into the darkness, too afraid to attack him. He strode forward.

The large monster spider turned his gaze on Caze. It had huge, inky-black eyes rimmed with yellow. It watched him, but kept spinning its cocoon around Lara.

Caze reached her. She was hanging off the ground, putting them face to face. He morphed his sword into a knife.

He attacked the web.

The spider shrieked and slammed a leg down right beside him.

He cursed and dodged. He moved right back to Lara, cutting through the tough web at her chest. The spider shrieked again and skittered backward, taking Lara with it. She cried out.

The spider kept wrapping web around her. It was up to her neck.

Caze moved forward, his gaze locking with Lara's. He was close enough to see the flash of fear in the blue depths.

"Caze..."

"Hold on, Lara." He cut into the web again. It was sticky and tough.

Suddenly, the spider's leg slammed down again. Caze's dodge was too slow this time. The furry leg hit his hip, sending him flying.

He landed on his side, pain flaring in his ribs. He'd cracked something. Sucking in a breath, he pushed back to his feet.

When he looked at Lara, his chest constricted. She was thrashing around, her face almost covered by the web.

"Lara!"

He sprinted toward her, and their gazes met. There was so much emotion churning in her eyes.

Before he reached her, the spider shifted and its leg slammed down again.

It knocked Caze off his feet. He hit the floor, skidding across the ground.

He went to rise, but the spider leg crashed down again. He rolled and the leg came down a hand's width from his face. *Boom*. The force of the blow dented the metal floor.

The leg lifted and as it raced downward again, Caze rolled.

Boom.

Again, it lifted and he rolled the other way.

Boom.

He rolled again. This time, he knocked into the small pack Lara had wrenched off her belt.

It held the three gems.

The spider skittered back, watching him. Lara made a noise and Caze looked at her. She jerked her eyes to her pack and then to him.

He shook his head. *No.* He wasn't going to leave her.

The spider let out a harsh noise. In a frenzy of spinning, it spewed more web on Lara. Caze's heart knocked against his ribs. The web now covered her nose.

"No." He surged upward.

Another leg slammed down and hit his arm. He heard the bone snap, pain like a sword cutting deep. The air rushed out of him.

"Cren." He cradled the arm to his chest and looked at Lara again.

Only her eyes were still left uncovered.

Lara.

Helplessness hit him like a weight. He couldn't get close enough to free her and even if he could, he needed time to cut through the web.

He glanced at the spider's inky-black eyes. Time he didn't have.

Hand shaking, he snatched up the pack with the gems.

He needed to regroup. He needed a plan. But every cell in his body did not want to leave her. In his head, he heard his father's voice telling him to complete his mission.

Then Lara's eyes closed and the web covered her head.

She was entirely encased in a web cocoon.

A wave of helpless fury washed over Caze. Pain ripped his insides to shreds and he let out a harsh roar.

The spider watched him with its soulless eyes.

Then turning, Caze ran from the room.

With every step, his helian pulsed with pain and sorrow.

Every step that took him farther away from Lara made the pain spike higher than anything he'd ever felt before.

CHAPTER SIXTEEN

L ara wanted to scream. She was trapped, she couldn't move, and as air sawed in and out of her lungs, she realized that it was getting harder and harder to breathe.

She still fought. That was all she knew—keep fighting until things got better. She fought with everything she had until she screamed in frustration.

She couldn't move. She was helpless.

The spider moved, lifting her. She gasped, trying to imagine what was happening. Then she was jerked to a stop.

Then...nothing.

Nothing but the sound of her own harsh breathing. A tear slipped down her cheek. Fucking Kantos. They stole everything, killed everything, destroyed everything.

Lara had found Caze. A magnificent warrior. A man who was so good, a man she was falling for.

Dammit, it wasn't fair that she had to die here.

But he'd gotten the gems. It was the last thing she'd seen—him snatching up the backpack.

He'd complete the mission. And he'd make sure that her sisters were safe.

Her death would not be in vain. She knew that her warrior would make the Kantos pay.

She pulled in a jerky breath. Her lungs were starting to burn.

Lara wanted to curl her fingers into her palms, but she couldn't even do that. Her heart stuttered.

So alone. Always alone.

As her oxygen-deprived mind wandered, she wished Caze hadn't left her. Like her dad had left her. Like her mother had abandoned her.

Except for her sisters, all the people she loved left her.

Love. Oh, God, she loved the big, bad warrior.

She heard a sound and sensed movement through the web. Her heart thudded. Was the spider back? Maybe now to finally eat her?

Lara squeezed her eyes closed harder. What did it matter? She was alone. So terribly alone. And she'd die soon anyway. Her lungs were burning, and she knew that she'd run out of air before much longer.

But she couldn't just stand there doing nothing. Even though it hurt, she struggled against the web.

Then she screamed as loudly as she could.

CREN. Caze spotted where the spider had slapped the freshly-made cocoon with Lara inside against the wall.

The creature had scuttled off into the darkness and, as he scanned the space, he counted dozens of other cocoons attached to the wall.

He barely controlled a shudder and forced himself to wait, even though every muscle in his body demanded he leap into action and tear her down. He had no idea how much time Lara had left.

But he couldn't help her if he was dead. He needed to make sure the spider had lost interest.

His broken arm throbbed. He'd aligned the bone as best he could and his helian was working overtime to repair it. It would hold for now, but another hit would shatter it.

Surrender. Give us the gems.

The guttural mental voice of an elite echoed in his head.

We are coming for you, warrior. You cannot escape.

The voice was the echo of several elites. *By Alqin's axe*, how many elites were on the station?

He gritted his teeth. It didn't matter if there were one or a hundred of them directing the soldiers and bugs. He didn't care. His mission be damned. He was saving Lara.

Caze moved. He couldn't see the spider. He snuck along the wall. He'd fight the entire hive station, every single Kantos they threw at him, to save Lara.

He'd fight as many elites as it took.

Her cocoon was well above the ground and he eyed the wall. It was rough, with small cavities and nooks peppered across it. He stuck a boot in one hole and climbed up.

Soon, he was level with Lara's cocoon. He connected with his helian and formed a knife.

Then Caze started cutting.

The web substance was sticky and tough, he locked his jaw and kept hacking, cutting, and slicing.

It was hard work and soon sweat dripped down his face. Did she still have air? He kept working, his heart thudding painfully.

He managed to make a small hole and he shoved his hand into it, gripping the edge of the cocoon. He heaved, tearing a chunk off.

He uncovered her face.

She was pale and she wasn't breathing. His pulse spiked. His helian didn't detect any life signs.

No, no, no.

"No, Lara." Wildly, he tore the cocoon. He got his knife inside and split the *cren*-cursed thing right down the middle.

Lara pitched forward and he caught her before she fell.

Holding her tightly to his chest, he climbed down. When his boots hit the floor, he swung her up and quickly carried her out of the spider's room. He wanted to get out of there before the monster realized one of its victims was missing.

The corridor was empty, and his throat was tight as he hurried to find a shadowed alcove.

He laid her flat on her back and pressed a palm to her chest. No movement.

Desperately, he pressed his mouth to hers, breathing air into her.

"Lara, please. Don't leave me." He kept breathing for her. He wanted her to sit up, curse the Kantos, demand retribution.

But she was so still. Lara being so still was wrong.

Caze kept breathing and pushing on her chest. Agony and despair chewed at him like acid. He couldn't lose her.

She'd become vital to him in just a few days.

The tough Terran never let anything stop her. She loved her sisters, and was a loyal, brilliant fighter, a generous lover.

And his. She was *his*.

"Breathe, Lara." He pressed his lips to hers and breathed. "*By Eschar*, breathe."

He thumped her chest.

"Breathe. Fight. You always fight."

He felt his helian flare and his palms warmed. He felt the jolt of the electric shock through his own body and Lara's.

Suddenly, her eyes opened, and she dragged in a breath. Then another. She sat up, coughing, and Caze tore her free from the last of the web stuck to her legs. He yanked her into his arms.

"Lara?" His pulse was racing and he felt lightheaded.

She sucked in more air, then her hands patted his cheeks. "Caze?"

Her voice was rough.

"I'm here."

"You...didn't leave me." She frowned. "The mission—"

"To borrow a phrase you've taught me, fuck the mission."

He saw a flicker of a smile on her face. Her hand moved, stroking along his jaw. "You're real?"

"Yes."

"We're alive?"

"Yes. For now. But we have to get to the ship."

"Right." She gave a fierce nod. "Well, help me up."

He did as ordered, but she was unsteady on her feet. Of course, her face was set to determined and stubborn, even as she wobbled. He knew she'd keep moving, no matter what.

Keeping one arm wrapped around her, Caze watched as she wavered, then locked her legs.

"Okay?" he asked.

"I am now. Anything is better than being in that cocoon." She shuddered.

He leaned down and kissed her. A soft, gentle kiss.

Her hand moved into his hair, tugging gently. She deepened the kiss and he savored the taste of her. She made a tiny sound in her throat.

She pressed her other palm to his chest, right over his heart. "Thanks for rescuing me, Caze."

"I'll always come for you, Lara."

You will die here.

The Kantos voice in their heads made them both stiffen.

We will pull out your entrails and feed them to our bugs.

"Yadda, yadda, yadda." Lara shook her head. "You think they get training to teach them to be assholes?"

"I suspect they come like that. We need to go." He helped her down the hall. "Are you okay to walk? I can carry you."

She snorted. "I'll walk." There was grit in her voice.

Caze couldn't help but smile. They walked down the corridor, and he knew that they'd have to fight their way out.

Clicking echoed behind them. He heard the Kantos soldiers coming.

Find them. Kill them.

Cren. He was agonizingly aware that Lara had no weapon. Still, she was Lara. Her body was a weapon.

"When they attack us, you stay behind me," he said.

"No."

He growled. "You're still unsteady and you don't have a weapon."

"No."

He wanted to roar with frustration. When your woman was a warrior, caring for her was hard.

Suddenly, she reached down and stroked his helian. He felt a throb of warmth, like it was focusing on her.

Then the black scales on his arm flowed over to her arm. Scale armor rolled up her arm and then spilled down her body.

"Oh, wow." Her eyes went wide.

The armor matched his—black scales with touches of silver. A sword, smaller than his but perfect for Lara, formed on her arm.

Caze felt a surge of fierce satisfaction. He liked

seeing her in his armor. He liked knowing that his helian accepted her.

Together, they would keep her safe.

"Come on," he urged. "The ship's close."

They rounded a corner...and came upon a wall of soldiers.

Cren. Their luck had run out.

There wasn't one, but six elites, flowing toward them on four legs.

Hand over the gems.

"No," Caze said.

"He means, hell no, bug face," Lara said.

Caze's lips quirked and he shook his head.

Give them to us. We are losing patience.

Lara cocked a hip. "Do we look like we care?"

The faces of the Kantos elites didn't change, but Caze got the impression the aliens were angry.

"Time to fight, hot stuff." She threw her arms out and her sword lengthened. She laughed, a deep, throaty sound. "Oh yeah, I like this." She fell into a fighting stance, and lifted her weapon. "Come on, bug boy. Let's dance."

CHAPTER SEVENTEEN

Lara and Caze tore through the Kantos soldiers.

Oh, she loved this armor and this sword. Lara spun and green blood flowed.

Caze fought like an avalanche—strong, powerful, and leaving a trail of destruction behind him.

She yanked her sword free of a bug and spun. She ended up back-to-back with Caze, slashing and stabbing.

"Lara."

He jerked his head. She saw the bug incoming. Caze leaned forward and she rolled over his back, and kicked the Kantos creature in the head.

She rolled back to her feet. They needed to get back to the ship. Get themselves and the gems to safety.

Caze slashed a gap through the line of soldiers. "Lara. Here!"

She dived, rolled, and knocked two soldiers over. She jumped up, skewering one through the gut with a grunt.

Caze's fingers closed over hers and they ran.

She hated leaving a fight, but she wanted *off* this hive

station. They dodged a bug and ran down another corridor.

All of a sudden, two flying bugs appeared, hovering in front of them. The damned things had huge, sharp stingers on their asses. The high-pitched buzzing sound they emitted made her ears ring.

One darted forward, jabbing its stinger at Lara.

She dodged to the side. Damn, she wished she had some of her throwing stars.

Like magic, two sharp, circular blades morphed on her sword arm. She grabbed them and held them up with a smile. They were perfectly formed and balanced.

Thank you, sweet helian. She threw the first, shifted, and threw the second one.

The first blade sliced off the tip of the stinger of the closest flying bug. Its buzzing went crazy, and it flew into the wall.

The second star sliced into the second bug's side. It darted sideways, buzzing madly.

"In here," Caze called out.

She saw him standing in the doorway to a side room. She jogged over and darted past him. He followed right behind her.

They didn't get far before they both jerked to a halt.

Oh, shit. There was a giant-ass centipede in the center of the room, with its hundreds of legs curled around a pile of purple eggs.

Caze held a finger to his lips. She nodded. *Right, don't wake the ugly creepy-crawly.*

They moved slowly, trying not to make a sound. The centipede moved, its legs twitching.

She froze and held her breath. They waited a beat, and then Caze waved his fingers.

Taking slow, deliberate steps, they neared the doorway on the far side of the room. Then, one of Lara's boots hit something on the floor, making a scraping noise.

The centipede's head shot up.

"Go!" Caze shoved her out the door.

She sprinted down the hall, Caze right behind her.

"I am *so* sick of bugs," she yelled.

"There are no bugs on the *Desteron*."

She glanced his way. "You inviting me to visit?"

Those black-and-silver eyes were unreadable, but she knew him well enough now to sense the emotion from him.

"Maybe. I'm sure your sister would like to see you."

Lara smiled. She could see straight through her warrior. "I think I'd like a visit to the premier Eon warship. As long as I don't end up in the brig."

"I know the head of security."

God, he made her want to laugh.

"Through there." He pointed through an archway. "We're close to our ship."

Yes. Elation burst inside her. They ducked through the narrow opening.

"Just down there." He nodded. "We're at the outer wall of the station."

They stopped and Caze touched the screen on his wrist. He moved a few steps, then pressed his palm to the wall. She watched the wall glow silver under his hand, the hole forming.

Then shock washed over Lara.

The helian had left the silver force field over the hole, but she could see through it clearly. Caze was silent a beat before he let out some vicious curses. He turned and slammed his boot into the wall.

The stealth ship was still there, but it was just a burned-out shell. One side of it was blown off, pieces floating in space.

"They found it," he said.

"Bastards." She turned to look at him. "We'll find a swarm ship. Escape that way."

"The swarm hangars are on the upper levels."

Every muscle in her body tensed. Right. And every bug and soldier on the station was between them and the swarm ships.

"We can't let them get the gems," he said quietly.

Lara nodded. That was unthinkable.

The distant echo of clicking and footsteps reached them. The Kantos were coming. A lot of them.

Caze pulled out the small pack. It bulged with the gems. Together, they checked the gems were secure. Then she saw something morph from his helian. It was a circular disc that glowed bright silver.

"What is it?"

"A tracker. The *Desteron* will be able to find it."

He set the tracker in the pack, ensured it was closed securely, then he tossed it through the force field covering the hole.

The field shimmered as the bag crossed it. Together, they stood, watching the pack float away into space.

"So, fancy a fight?" she asked.

He turned to her, the ends of his mouth tipping up. "Perhaps."

She lifted her sword arm. "Be a shame not to use this awesome armor and kick-ass sword some more."

"And you use them so well. You're unlike any woman I've ever known, Lara." He cupped the side of her face.

She savored the warmth of him and wished he wasn't wearing gloves. "I thought I was infuriating?"

"You're that, too."

She smiled, moving closer to him. The tips of their boots touched. "Caze, you should probably know that—" she drew in a deep breath "—I'm falling in love with you."

Something flickered in his eyes. "Love?"

God, she finally dredged up the courage to tell the man, to take a risk and he looked...confused.

"Forget it—"

He gripped her shoulders. "I don't know anything about love." He slid his hand up into her hair. "I wish I did. I...feel so many confusing, amazing things when I'm with you."

The air rushed out of her. He'd been raised by a hard, warrior father and devoted himself to being the perfect warrior.

"I'm no expert either," she whispered. "I wish we had more time."

"As do I." He pressed his lips to hers, his tongue delving into her mouth.

The kiss was over too quickly.

She gripped him. "I'm glad they sent you to hunt me down, Caze Vann-Jad."

"Me too, Lara Traynor."

Then, Kantos soldiers streamed into the corridor.

CAZE TURNED and lifted his weapon.

He didn't know anything about love, but there was a fierce mix of emotions storming through him. Lara was his, and he would do anything to protect her.

She gave him a bold smile, then together they charged into the approaching Kantos.

They fought. Their swords sliced and swung. Despite the tight confines of the tunnel, they cut through the first wave of soldiers.

But Caze knew they wouldn't leave the hive station alive.

"Fuck you." Lara sliced an arm off a soldier. She snatched the severed limb and threw it at the staggering alien.

All fighters, converge on the intruders.

Caze ignored the rasping voices in his head and kept fighting. But as more Kantos—of all shapes and sizes—poured into the corridor, he knew that they couldn't fight all of them.

They couldn't keep this up forever.

Do not kill them. I want them as prisoners.

Caze's chest tightened. If the Kantos captured them, he knew they'd torture Lara endlessly to get him to tell them where the gems were.

He wouldn't let that happen.

Ever.

"Lara."

"What?" She swung her sword out to the side, her feet spread for balance. Then she thrust a leg forward and kicked a bug away.

"We can't fight them all," he said.

She dragged in a breath. "I know."

He slashed with his blade, slicing open a small, furry bug. Then he glanced at the hole out into space, before meeting her gaze again.

She looked at the hole, realization crossing her face.

Sharp, black projectiles peppered the wall between them. Caze jumped back, but one clipped Lara, spinning her around.

"Shit." She slapped a hand over her arm. "I'm okay. Just grazed me." She pulled in a breath. "I'm up for a romantic spacewalk, hot stuff."

This woman. Courage and steel.

He grabbed her hand, and his sword morphed to a blaster. As they moved toward the hole, he fired on the Kantos to drive them back.

His helian morphed space helmets for them, the thin, clear covering sliding over their faces. He nodded at her, then fired on the Kantos again. Lara turned and dived through the hole. No hesitation.

Caze got off another round of laser fire, then dived after her.

She was right in front of him and he grabbed her hand. They pushed off the side of the station, passing through the debris of their ship.

"I'm sorry this mission didn't end better," he said.

She smiled. "The gems aren't in the Kantos' hands.

You and I are together." Her fingers squeezed his. "I'm pretty happy with that."

"I..." He cleared his throat. "If we made it back, I would have liked you to teach me about love."

"I've never had much experience with it myself. Watching my mother's struggle, I guess I saw a bad example of it." Lara gripped him tighter. "Now I know that love, the real thing, makes you stronger. It nourishes you, sets you free."

He pulled her closer, their helmets clunking together. He could see the blue of her eyes. "We could have learned together."

She cupped a hand to the side of his helmet. "Whatever or wherever we end up, I'll find you, Caze. This life, the next, heaven, hell, Valhalla."

He didn't know all the words, but he understood the meaning.

"I realize now that I'm not like my mom. I'd prefer to have love, for even a short time, than never have felt it at all. Never have had you in my life."

"*Cren*, Lara." He tightened his hold on her and his helian pulsed.

Then he felt an impact on his back and searing pain. He jolted.

"Caze!"

More projectiles fired past them. Another hit his shoulder and he grunted.

"Fuck, they're shooting at us." She turned him frantically.

Then a projectile hit her and she cried out. The slim bolt had pierced her arm.

ANNA HACKETT

No. Caze wrapped his arms around her, turning his back to the hive. He wouldn't let them hurt her.

"Caze—"

He commanded his helian, and a burst of propulsion from the symbiont sent them flying away from the station.

More projectiles peppered his back, his body jolting with each hit. Pain rolled through him and Lara cried out. His head was turning foggy and he felt blood pooling inside his armor.

"Lara... Mine. My mate."

"Caze." She pressed closer. "Hold on, warrior."

"Protect...you."

Another projectile hit him and Lara screamed.

"No!"

Then, with the feel of his mate against him, Caze lost consciousness.

CHAPTER EIGHTEEN

Lara could barely breathe. Caze was slumped against her.

She felt another jolt hit his body, knew another projectile had torn into him. A tear slid down her cheek.

He'd shielded her. Was still shielding her and taking hits to keep her safe.

No one had ever protected her like that before. Most people in her life expected her to keep them safe.

They drifted away from the hive station, and soon, the projectiles stopped. She let out a shuddering breath. They were out of range.

She knew Caze was bleeding. She felt his chest rising with short, shallow breaths.

The best, most magnificent man she'd ever met, the man she was falling in love with, was dying in her arms.

She screamed in her helmet at the helplessness. Then she felt him stir against her, agitated, and realized she was upsetting him.

"Shh." She smoothed a hand down his arm, careful

not to touch where a projectile protruded from his bicep.

She started to sing a Japanese lullaby that her Grandmother Kimiko had sung to her as a little girl, back when things were still happy in the Traynor family. It was about sunny days and green grass, cherry blossoms and laughter.

She and Caze hadn't had any of that in their lives. Sunny days and laughter. She felt a pain in her arm where a projectile had clipped her, but ignored it. She poured everything she felt into the song.

Lara pulled him closer. She wasn't letting go. Even when her arms started to ache, she held tight. She lost track of time, her throat turning raw from the singing.

She wasn't sure how much longer the helian could supply air for her. And any second, she expected swarm ships to surround them.

Caze's helian was trying to heal him, she could sense it. But she also knew it was failing. Her warrior was dying.

She kept singing, her voice turning hoarse. God, she would have loved a lifetime of adventures with him.

More minutes passed, and she suddenly realized she couldn't feel his chest rising and falling anymore. The agony made her bite her tongue. Her throat was so tight.

Silent tears streamed down her face.

"I'm sorry, Caze."

Then brilliant lights speared into her eyes.

Lara blinked. A ship was approaching. Her stomach dropped. The Kantos had found them.

Holding a hand up against the light, she stared, her vision slowly adjusting.

The hull of a huge, black ship was heading toward them.

A scaled hull.

Her chest hitched. An Eon warship.

"Lara, hold on. We're coming." Eve's urgent voice rang in Lara's helmet.

She saw a flare of light as a side door opened on the ship. Two large, muscular silhouettes, wearing black-scale armor and helmets, pushed off. They kept their arms by their sides, flying toward her.

"Help's here, Caze." Her voice was a croak. "Your warriors are here."

"Lara?" Eve's voice.

"Hey, sis."

"Hold on."

Lara let out a wet laugh. "I'm not going anywhere."

Then Eve cursed. "Davion, we have swarm ships incoming. Hold tight, Lara. Davion will bring you aboard."

Lara turned her head to look away from the *Desteron*. In the distance, hundreds of shapes filled her vision. Swarm ships raced toward them from the hive station.

Suddenly, a squadron of sleek, black fighters shot out of the side of the *Desteron*. Lara gasped at the sight as they whizzed overhead.

They all had strips of glowing blue and silver light on them. The Eon fighters raced toward the swarm ships. Lasers lit up the blackness of space.

"Lara."

The deep voice made her look back. The two warriors had reached them.

Through the helmet of the closest warrior, she saw a sharply masculine face. The "man in charge" vibe throbbed off him, even through his armor.

"War Commander Thann-Eon."

He smiled. "Davion, remember?"

Then his gaze swiveled to Caze hanging in her arms, and his smile vanished.

"He's badly hurt—" her voice broke. "Please. Please help him."

The other warrior moved up close. He gripped Caze's arms, but Lara couldn't make her fingers let go.

"My name is Brack," the warrior said. "I'm Davion's second-in-command. We'll take care of Caze."

But Lara still couldn't let go. If she held on, she could still pretend he was with her, that he was okay.

Brack looked over at Davion. "I'm not detecting any life signs—"

Lara cried out, a terrible sob catching in her chest.

"Brack." Davion's tone held a sharp warning. "Lara, we need to get him to medical."

She swallowed and looked at Brack. She remembered she'd seen him before on screen. She couldn't tell what color the strands in his eyes were.

"I'm his friend," Brack assured her.

"He mentioned you. Said you were annoying."

She felt a throb of emotion from the warrior. "He can be equally exasperating."

Davion's arms wrapped around her from behind. "Let go, Lara."

She forced herself to let Caze go.

Brack gripped Caze under the arms, turned, and

zoomed back to the ship with a blast of propulsion from his helian.

Taking Caze away from her.

Lara tried to control her tears and failed. Gently, Davion maneuvered her so he had one arm wrapped around her.

"Hold on."

She nodded dully. They flew back toward the *Desteron*.

Ahead, she saw Brack enter the airlock.

A sob escaped. "Sorry, I never cry."

"I've heard this before."

"Eve's lying. She cries when she watches horror movies. It's so weird." But Lara couldn't force a smile. "He protected me."

Davion's gaze dropped to her scale armor. "And he shared his helian with you."

She bit on her lip to fight the pain. "Yes."

They reached the *Desteron* and Davion helped her inside.

Then Lara saw Eve waiting for them.

Something broke inside Lara. Her helmet retracted and she fell into her sister's arms.

CAZE WOKE WITH A ROAR. Sitting up, he tore at the tubes sticking into his body.

"Take it easy," a deep voice said. "Calm down."

Confused, his brain struggled to pull everything together. He sucked in a deep breath, fighting for some control. His helian was throbbing—not in pain, but clearly agitated.

Caze felt a heavy hand on his shoulder and he turned, snarling. Memories of agony washed over him. Projectiles hitting his body.

"Caze, it's Aydin."

Caze stared at the strands of green in the man's dark eyes.

"You're in medical on the *Desteron*."

Desteron.

Caze reached up, touching his shoulder, then his chest, his side.

"You were badly injured," Aydin continued, the doctor checking a screen attached to the bunk. "Your helian had shut down almost all your body's systems. We thought we'd lost you."

Pushing through the fog in his head, Caze tried to remember what had happened. There was something. Something important that he was missing.

"I removed the Kantos projectiles. Your body had partially healed around them and—"

In the background, Aydin's voice turned to a drone. Kantos projectiles.

Caze sucked in a breath.

Lara. *Lara.* His mate.

He swung his legs off the bed. Machines beeped angrily.

Aydin cursed. "Take it easy."

"Where's Lara?"

The doctor smiled. "I see the important things are coming back to you."

Caze felt something rising inside him, hot and urgent. He *needed* to see his woman. "She's okay?"

"She's fine. She's been by your bedside ever since she came aboard. Only Eve's bullying got her to shower and let me treat her injuries."

"Injuries?" Caze pushed to his feet, and dizziness swamped him. He clamped a hand on the edge of the bunk to stay upright.

Aydin huffed out a breath, gripping Caze's arm. "Her injuries were minor. She's fully healed. I don't suppose I can convince you to get back in the bed."

Caze just shot the doctor a look.

"Right." Aydin started removing the remaining tubes in Caze's skin. "Eve and Davion ordered Lara to the bridge. They needed her assistance with recovering the gems. She and Eve are also working to find her sister and the *Rengard*."

Caze grunted. He wouldn't feel better until he saw her with his own eyes. "Did they locate the *Rengard*?"

"Not yet. Davion did manage to get a partial message through to War Commander Dann-Jad. Eve and Lara are hoping enough information made it through that he doesn't kill their sister. It appears she still has control of the warship."

Caze grunted again. Nothing about the Traynor sisters surprised him anymore. "And the gems?"

"We should almost be at their location." Aydin shook his head. "I can't believe you tossed the sacred gems of the warriors into space."

"At the time, my options were limited." Caze felt the *Cren*-cursed dizziness clearing. Once he was sure that his legs would hold him, he let go of the bed. "I need to get to Lara."

Aydin rolled his eyes and ran a scanner over Caze. "Everyone around here seems to forget that I'm the doctor. I'm the one that clears patients to return to their duties."

Caze raised a brow. "Are you finished?"

The doctor's face changed and he stared at the scanner. His head snapped up. *"By Eschar's bow,* you're entering the mating fever."

Caze smiled. The mating fever was intense. An Eon male would keep his mate for days of sex and bonding.

Aydin stared at Caze with a stunned expression. "You're *smiling.*"

"My mate makes me smile. She makes me laugh." Caze strode toward the door. He wasn't waiting another ship minute to get his hands on his woman. "I'm going to find her."

The doctor let out a choked laugh. "Ah, perhaps before you head to the bridge, you should put some clothes on."

Caze looked down. He was completely naked, with a rampant erection. "Perhaps."

Aydin laughed again, heading for a supply cupboard.

Soon, Caze was striding down the *Desteron*'s corridors, headed for the bridge. He wore a pair of black trousers, but hadn't wasted time pulling on a shirt.

Several warriors in black uniform spotted him, moving to the side and standing to attention. Caze didn't slow down, just nodded at them.

Then he saw the double doors to the bridge. Anticipation licked at his insides. Lara was in there. The doors slid open.

The *Desteron's* bridge had multiple tiers, ringed by workstations manned by warriors. Caze ignored them all. His gaze went straight to the dark-haired woman standing in front of the large viewscreen.

She was standing beside Davion and Eve.

They turned.

Eve smiled and Davion studied Caze intently, then his shoulders relaxed.

Lara stared straight at him, her eyes widening and her lips tilting up. Her gaze moved over his bare chest and he could see the hunger ignite in her eyes.

He watched her shift her feet. He knew that she was feeling the edge of the mating fever, too.

"You're okay," she murmured.

Then he saw something else he never expected to from his tough warrior. A sheen of tears in her eyes.

Caze strode to her. There was so much emotion on her face and he felt the echo of it in his chest.

"Caze," Davion said. "I'm very happy to see you up and healed. We're following the tracker you placed on the gems—"

For the first time ever, Caze ignored his war commander. He didn't give a *cren* about the gems.

He swept Lara into his arms, yanking her off her feet. She made a small sound of surprise, then she threw her arms around his neck and clamped her legs around his hips.

"Hey there, hot stuff," she whispered.

He kissed her. He didn't hesitate or make it soft. No,

it was hot and hard, and he poured all of his emotions into it.

She moaned into his mouth and he drank her up. They were alive. They were together. And that was the only thing that mattered in Caze's world.

He pressed his face to her hair and breathed in her scent.

The bridge was silent. He glanced up and saw warriors staring, their mouths hanging open. A smiling Davion had an arm around Eve.

Then Lara cupped Caze's cheek. "Caze?" She stroked his skin. "You're truly okay, baby?"

"Yes. I'm completely healed."

Her lips trembled. "You were hurt so badly—"

"I'm not now."

"You shielded me." Her voice was a soft whisper.

"And I'd do it again." He pressed his forehead to hers. "I would die for you."

"Please, don't." Her voice cracked. "I held you for hours, not knowing if you were still alive."

Warmth filled his chest. "You didn't let go. You held on to me."

"Always."

Caze tightened his hold on her, then looked at Davion. "If you need me, my mate and I will be in my cabin."

Lara gasped and lowered her voice. "Warrior, you just told everyone we're going to have sex."

"Yes. A lot of it."

He strode off the bridge, Davion's laughter echoing after them.

CHAPTER NINETEEN

S he was about to come.

Lara drove down on Caze's cock, sensations ricocheting inside her.

"Get there, my mate," he growled.

They were face-to-face in the center of his bed. She was riding him hard, and he was still being bossy.

"I'll get there when I'm ready." She rose up and slammed down, filling herself with him again. Her moan echoed around them.

Her big, strong, protective warrior filled her up. His groan was long and loud. Music to her ears.

His hands slid down between their bodies. He touched where they were joined, where his cock was buried inside her.

"You're stretched so prettily around me, Lara. My big cock making your body work to take me."

God, she loved when her usually stoic mate talked dirty. She lifted up and sank back down again. "I'm taking you just fine, hot stuff. I'll take everything you've got to give me."

She moved faster, and Caze found her clit, working it with his thumb.

She was whimpering now and she didn't care one little bit. "Yes, baby. Don't stop."

Her orgasm hit her like a detonation. She slammed down, a strangled cry ripping from her.

Caze groaned, thrusting his hips up. His hands clamped on her hips.

Lara felt his helian flare and was hit with an intoxicating mix of both her pleasure and Caze's. A second orgasm hit her by surprise, her body clamping down on his cock. She cried out.

"*Cren.*" He reared up, shoving her back.

She found herself on her back, her warrior above her. His face was fierce as he pistoned into her.

A moment later, he found his own release. He groaned, body shuddering as he came hard, jetting inside her.

When he collapsed, he made sure he fell right beside her and not on top of her. He did that every time. He was well aware of his strength and size, and he always made sure he didn't crush her.

Lara pulled in a deep breath, snuggling against his damp skin. "That was amazing, baby."

He lifted his head. He had a very satisfied look on his face.

She reached up and tugged on his hair. "God, I love your hair."

"I noticed. You like to yank on it when I'm licking

those pretty folds between your legs." His voice was deep and lazy.

She tugged on it again, making a mock angry face at him.

He smiled at her. A big, wide, beautiful smile.

Her heart squeezed. He was alive. Her warrior was gorgeously alive.

And he'd been proving it for the last two days. They'd been locked in his cabin—eating, drinking, having sex, and making love.

They'd had plenty of amazing, no-holds-barred fucking. She snuggled deeper, absorbing the warmth of him. But there had also been plenty of sweet lovemaking. Slow, lazy, and glorying in their connection.

He spoiled her with all kinds of tasty foods. Many of which she'd smeared on his body and licked off his skin, a pleasurable experience for both of them. The washroom was overflowing with all the lotions and scents he'd synthesized for her. It appeared her warrior enjoyed spoiling her.

Lara pressed her cheek to his chest. She heard the strong, steady thud of his heart.

"I thought you were dead," she whispered.

His arms tightened on her.

"We floated in space for hours." All the pain and fear rushed back. "I couldn't tell if you were breathing."

"*Shara*..." His hands slid up her back. "I'm fine."

"When Davion and Brack arrived, Brack said he couldn't detect your life signs."

"Because Brack has a big mouth and talks before he

thinks. My helian had slowed everything down to keep me alive."

She pressed into him. "I thought I'd lost you. Before I really even had you."

"I'm right here, *shara*."

"What does *shara* mean?"

"It is what the warrior Alqin called his mate Eschar. His love, his woman."

She tugged on his hair. "How many women have you whispered it to before me?"

"No one. Only you."

Her belly quivered. "I love you, Caze. I'm going to teach you what love means, but I think you're off to a pretty good start." She kissed his pec. "I'm going to show you how good we can be together."

He smiled, fiddling with her hair. "There's no need for you to prove anything to me. I love you too, Lara."

Warmth flared in her belly. "But you—"

He tugged her up, his lips finding hers. This kiss wasn't fueled by the frenzy of the mating fever. This was a long, slow kiss. They took their time.

When he lifted his lips from hers, they were both breathing heavily.

"I didn't know what love was," he said. "But when I look at you, what I feel for you... I know what love feels like now, Lara mine. I know how it feels to mate, to protect a woman, to shield her, make her happy, see her smile, hear her cry my name in pleasure."

Lara bit her lip. God, what had happened to the stern warrior she'd first faced across a temple courtyard? "Caze."

"Are you mine, Lara Traynor of Earth? My woman, my warrior, my lover, my mate?"

"Yes, Caze Vann-Jad. I'm yours and you're mine. My warrior, my man, my lover, my hot stuff."

He rolled on top of her, his mouth taking hers again. "Show me."

Wren

SHIT, *shittity, shit.*

Wren Traynor ran through the narrow maintenance conduit. She heard the rumble of voices—deep, male voices—reverberating from nearby.

She ducked into a small alcove. In the pitch darkness, she dropped to her knees, pushed open a small panel, and crawled in. She fitted the panel back into place, and turned to face the tiny space that had been her hidey-hole for the last few days.

Dropping to her butt, she leaned against the metallic wall and sighed.

She was tired. Stressed out. And she didn't smell very good.

That's what happens when you hijack an alien warship, Wren.

God, her life sucked. She let her head thunk back against the wall. One day, she'd been working at her tech company, creating amazing, cutting-edge programs and being a badass with a keyboard. At night, she'd done some...creative hacking. Just to keep herself busy and her skills sharp.

Then, just over five months ago, things had gone sideways. Her sister, Eve, had been imprisoned for a crime she hadn't committed. Wren still felt the wild rush of anger at the injustice of it all.

She pushed her mass of dark curls back over her shoulder. She winced. Her hair was greasy as hell. *Gah*. She needed a shower and would sell her soul for one. Wet wipes weren't cutting it anymore.

Sighing, she pulled her tablet out. The screen glowed, lighting up the small space around her. She'd been damn grateful to find this space. Tucked between some internal maintenance access conduits, she was pretty sure the warriors didn't know it existed.

She stroked her tablet. Her baby. She'd built the device herself. It had top-of-the-line, experimental components.

With it, and her mad skills, she'd managed to sneak aboard an Eon warship, take over their systems, and take control of the ship.

She'd then spent four days sending them jumping around distant space.

The ship's war commander and his crew had been working tirelessly to find her. Wren had spent that time ensuring they didn't, usually by creating havoc on the ship and keeping them busy.

She needed to get the warship to the rendezvous point with Earth's Space Corps. Her sister's freedom depended on it. The survival of Earth depended on it. How the Space Corps planned to subdue an entire ship of pissed off Eon warriors, she had no clue. She didn't care. Her job was to get the *Rengard* to the rendezvous.

Wren rubbed her brow. She had a headache forming. She rifled through her backpack and pulled out some food packs and water.

Somehow, War Commander Dann-Jad had disabled the ship's star drive. They were now stuck at standard speed.

It was going to be a long trip to the rendezvous. She'd run out of food and water far before then. Which was no doubt what the war commander had in mind.

She munched on the bland rations, dreaming of a thick, juicy steak. And a slice of cheesecake. Fresh strawberries. So, she could either die of thirst and starvation, or she could die at the hands of an angry Eon war commander who'd likely wring her neck. And take pleasure in doing it.

Hmm. Choices, choices.

She tossed the empty wrapper in her backpack. This was why she preferred her computer lab to spending time with people. In her lab, she was queen of her domain, and the few people she allowed in were awed by her crazy-good skills.

Wren thumbed her tablet screen, and a picture of her with her sisters appeared. *Eve and Lara.* Love filled Wren. She was the baby, and her sisters had always protected her, looked out for her.

In the picture, her sisters had Wren squeezed in between them. Wren was laughing, Lara had an arm outstretched to take the picture. Eve was smirking and looking badass. It was over a year old, on the last vacation the three of them had managed to take. They'd sunned themselves on a beach in the Caribbean, and the rest of the time, Wren had fought their attempts to make her go parasailing and jet-skiing.

Her sisters were both taller and more athletic than Wren. They both loved space and fighting. Both were tough, accomplished, and badass.

And then there was Wren. Her nose wrinkled. She was shorter and curvier, with five pounds she couldn't shift. Okay, so she had a serious chocolate and latte addiction that she had no intention of giving up. And she didn't exercise—she shuddered—unless she had to.

She touched the image of Eve's face. God, she prayed her sister was okay. The Space Corps had forced her on a dangerous mission to abduct an Eon war commander. Air whistled through Wren's teeth. And not any Eon war commander, the deadliest one.

Not that War Commander Malax Dann-Jad was a slouch. The man was proving *way* more intelligent than she'd assumed.

The Space Corps had approached Wren and offered her a deal too. Hijack the Eon warship, the *Rengard*, and they'd recall Wren's sister and grant Eve her freedom.

God, her sister Lara would be going crazy with worry for Eve and not knowing where Wren was.

And here she was. Stuck in the bowels of an alien ship while its war commander tore it apart to find her.

Suddenly, her tablet screen went black, plunging her into darkness. She frowned.

Then words appeared on the screen.

Terran.

Her eyebrows rose. He'd hacked her tablet? The prick. Her fingers flew.

She and the war commander had traded a few messages over the last few days. But they were messages *she'd* sent him when she'd tapped his system. He did *not* get to hack her baby.

Wren quickly checked her system and released a breath. They didn't have a lock on her location.

She replied. *War Commander.*

Earth now has an alliance with the Eon. Stand down.

What? Wren chewed her lip, studying the words suspiciously.

She tapped the screen. *I don't believe you.*

Stubborn woman. Your sister brokered a deal.

Wren chewed on her lip hard enough to wince. Could it be true? Was Eve okay?

Return control of my ship.

His anger practically throbbed off the screen. She didn't need to be anywhere near the man to know he was pissed to the *nth* degree.

She'd seen a photo of him. Eon warriors all looked similar—big and muscled, long hair framing rugged faces. They all had hair in shades of brown. But there was something a little harsher about Malax Dann-Jad. The firm line of his square jaw, or maybe the scowl she suspected was his permanent expression.

She tapped her screen. *No.*

She suspected the war commander would do just about anything to get her to surrender control of his ship. Including lie to her.

You will regret your actions.

Wren snorted. *I already do, but I have no choice.*

There is always a choice, Terran. Relinquish control and turn yourself in. I can assure your safety.

Another snort. *Yeah, right.*

Woman, do not test me. You won't like the consequences.

Okay, Wren felt a little tremor in her belly. She never, ever wanted to come face-to-face with War Commander Dann-Jad.

Don't threaten me. I haven't had a latte in days, and my chocolate stash ran out a long time ago.

The screen stayed blank, and she figured he wasn't quite sure what to make of her.

Last chance. Surrender.

Annoying man. *You can't see me right now, but I'm poking my tongue out at you. I don't follow your orders, War Commander.*

Wren tapped the screen, found the command she wanted, and hit it. Right now, lights were turning off across the entire ship.

It was childish, but she couldn't help herself.

Woman.

Just that single word on the screen. Wren imagined she could hear the war commander's angry roar from here.

Game on, War Commander.

CHAPTER TWENTY

"I want you to run another check on the Tarrant-class missiles," Caze said. "And Halon, good job with the upgrades to the pulse cannon array."

The warrior straightened. "Thank you, Security Commander."

Caze scanned his security team. "Any sign of the *Rengard* on scans?"

The warriors shook their heads.

Cren. He'd been hoping to give Lara some good news about her sister.

He nodded to his team and left the security room. He strode onto the bridge and his gaze went straight to Lara.

She looked over her shoulder and winked at him. She looked very fine in her black *Desteron* uniform.

He smiled. He was happy. He'd been content with his life before, dedicated to his work. But now he was happy in a way he'd never felt before.

On the central table on the bridge sat the three gems

of the first warriors. They'd successfully recovered them all.

Davion turned. "King Gayel has been briefed that the gems are okay."

"So, he has his war commander and his gems back," Eve said.

"Now we just need his warship." Davion crossed his arms over his chest.

Lara held Caze's gaze. "Update on the *Rengard*?"

He shook his head. "Still no sign of it."

She cursed. "Damn."

Eve turned to the viewscreen. "Where is she?"

Lara grabbed her sister's hand. "We'll find her. Then I'll wring her neck for ever agreeing to this."

Eve pressed into Lara's side. "You know she can't turn down a challenge."

Caze moved to his mate. She released her sister, and planted her face into his chest. He hugged her tight.

He felt the scrutiny from the warriors on the bridge. They were still adjusting to Caze and Davion being mated and openly showing affection.

He felt his helian beat. It felt so right, and he didn't care what anyone thought. Although he'd yet to apprise his father of his mated status. He cleared his throat. Maybe after they'd recovered the *Rengard*.

"You spoke with the Space Corps?" he asked.

Lara lifted her head. "Yes. I'm on a leave of absence."

He nodded.

"And I ripped Admiral Barber a new one. Sending Wren, of all people, into a dangerous situation." Lara growled.

Caze smoothed a hand down her hair. He'd learned when Lara got angry it was best to let her get it out. Or help her burn it off.

She sucked in a breath. "Davion has assigned me to train the *Desteron*'s warriors in Earth-style fighting."

Caze stiffened, but she didn't seem to notice.

"Eve's been teaching a few classes, so I'm going to take over for her so she can focus on her very important ambassador duties."

From nearby, Eve lifted a finger at her sister.

Lara grinned. "I'm going to add a few classes of my own, as well."

Caze's head was bombarded with images of Lara wrestling with warriors on the mats in the gym. It made him scowl.

Her grin widened. "Don't worry, hot stuff, I'll beat their asses."

"Maybe I'm worried about their asses, not yours." He slid a hand down over the aforementioned ass.

She shot him a look and moved his hand back to her waist. "My ass is just fine, thank you."

"It sure is."

"So." She paused. "I had a warrior tell me I could have assigned quarters—"

Caze growled. "My mate sleeps with me."

She patted his chest. "That's what I told him."

Caze wanted to kiss her. Right here on the bridge. Better yet, he wanted to drag her back to their cabin and strip that uniform off her.

Like she read his mind, she leaned in, her voice a

whisper. "How about I meet you back at our place for a lunch-break quickie?"

His cock was hard in an instant. "I love you."

"I love you too, hot stuff." She pulled back and winked. "See you in an hour."

Before her, Caze's life had been endless work. Pleasure had never, ever been a priority. He watched his mate walk away, his gaze dropping to her rounded ass in her uniform.

For the first time in his life, he was looking forward to more. He couldn't wait to see where life with his Terran mate took him.

***

LARA TILTED her head up under the misty shower spray. She had the temperature set to hot, and it felt good. She had a few bruises and sore muscles from her first training session with the warriors. God, she missed having a bath.

She'd set a few cocky Eon hotshots on their asses. She smiled. Of course, some of her aches were from her energetic and very pleasurable lunch date with her own warrior.

She quickly finished bathing and dressed. She was meeting Eve. Then they had dinner plans with Davion and Caze. Caze was currently off on some mysterious errand he was very cagey about.

She found Eve in a large room at the bow of the *Desteron*. Lara gasped. A huge window gave a beautiful view of space and the stars sprinkling across it like diamond chips. There were several benches and low chairs. The space looked like some sort of lounge.

Except for Eve, it was empty. Lara guessed Eon warriors didn't lounge around doing nothing very often.

Eve walked over, her damp hair in a ponytail. She moved with her usual quick, athletic stride.

Lara smiled, feeling a rush of love. She'd missed her sister. She hugged Eve close.

"Going gooey on me?" Eve asked.

Lara punched her sister's arm. "Just happy you're okay."

Eve grabbed her hand. "I'm really glad you're okay, too."

Then the happiness dimmed. *Wren.* Things wouldn't be completely right until they found their sister.

"She'll be okay." Eve pulled back, doing some sisterly mind reading. "She's insanely smart."

Lara dragged a hand through her hair. "Too smart, sometimes. She can also be clueless. And reckless." Lara groaned. "I can't believe she hijacked an Eon warship."

"A ship full of warriors."

Lara's heart thudded. "These warriors are tough, Eve. When Caze and I first clashed, we did not go easy on each other."

"I have to believe they won't hurt her," Eve said. "These warriors are tough, but they're noble and protective, as well."

Lara hoped Eve was right. "You happy?"

Eve smiled. It was the biggest smile Lara had seen on

her sister since they'd lost their dad so long ago. "I'm insanely happy. Davion is..."

When her sister's voice trailed off, Lara nodded. "Yeah. I know exactly what you mean."

"I never thought about love, Lara. Never found anyone who made me feel anything remotely like Dav does." She paused. "A part of me always worried that if I did find someone, that they'd leave me. Like Dad. Like Mom."

Lara nodded. "And I *never* wanted anything to do with love. After watching Mom—"

"You are *not* Mom," Eve said emphatically.

"I know. But seeing what love did to her, how it messed her up, I just always thought love wasn't worth the risk."

"And now?"

"Caze is worth anything."

Eve smiled, shaking her head. "The Traynor sisters in love."

"Who would have thought? Wren will find it highly amusing."

"She will." Eve's smile faded. "But we still have to deal with the Kantos."

"Fucking Kantos."

Eve's face hardened. "We find Wren, then we show those bugs that they picked the wrong damn planet to invade."

"Hell, yeah." Lara looked forward to kicking some more Kantos ass. "And the Eon king is committed to helping us?"

"The new king is doing things his way. Dav assures me that he's a good man. He's made a treaty with us—"

"And made you Ambassador Eve Thann-Eon."

Eve groaned. "Yeah, don't remind me." Then a wicked grin crossed her face. "You realize that you're now Lara Vann-Jad."

Lara's mouth dropped open. *Hell.*

Eve bumped her shoulder against Lara's before her face turned serious again. "With the Kantos attacking Davion and then stealing the sacred gems, King Solann-Eon is furious. He, Davion, and I'm sure Caze, are pretty damn motivated to shut the Kantos down."

Good. Lara stared out at space. With the full might of the Eon Empire behind them, they could do this.

Again, her thoughts turned to Wren. *We'll find you, Wrenny.*

The door opened and Davion and Caze strode in.

Lara's gaze went straight to her man. God, he was so delicious.

"We're so damn lucky," Eve murmured, her gaze locked on her mate.

"I never thought we'd meet men like them."

"Smart, easy on the eyes, good in a fight," Eve said.

"And damn good between the sheets. And on them."

The sisters laughed.

The men's gazes sharpened on them. As Lara watched Caze stride toward her, she saw a man who loved all the parts of her—both the soft and the sharp ones. A man who respected her, supported her, loved her.

Eve was right. They were so damn lucky.

Caze wrapped his arms around her. "The look on your face is worrying me."

Lara smiled. "Nothing to worry about, hot stuff. Just admiring my mate."

There was a flash in his eyes. "I heard you left some warriors grumbling and tending their injuries."

"They underestimated me."

Caze smiled. "Then they deserved their bruises."

"I seem to recall that you underestimated me once or twice."

"I learned my lesson." He stroked his fingers along her jaw. "I won't make the same mistake again."

"Where have you been?"

"Organizing a little surprise for my mate."

Another gift? She smiled. "More lotion? Some new, scrumptious foods for me to try? Not more clothes, I hope. Our closet is already bulging. I don't need more robes or lingerie, Caze."

"Davion and Brack helped me install a bathtub in our washroom."

Her mouth opened, then closed. Damn, she felt a burn in her eyes. Her mate, a man raised to be a warrior to the exclusion of all else, had just installed a bath tub for her on a warship. "I love you."

He smiled. "I know." He stroked her cheek. "I know you love having a bath and have been missing it."

"You're stuck with me now, Caze."

"Then it is a good thing I love you and I'm never going to let you go."

"That's lucky, hot stuff. Because I'm holding onto you forever."

Her mate wrapped his arms around her tighter and leaned down to kiss her. "Forever."

It could be a day, a year, or a lifetime, and it didn't matter. She knew their love was a solid, steady thing that would never break. It would sustain and support them.

As Caze's mouth meshed with hers, it made Lara realize just what forever felt like.

I hope you enjoyed Lara and Caze's story!

Eon Warriors continues with *Heart of Eon* starring computer expert Wren Traynor as she faces off with the Eon warrior whose warship she's hijacked, War Commander Malax Dann-Jad. **Read on for a preview of the first chapter.**

Don't miss out! For updates about new releases, action romance info, free books, and other fun stuff, sign up for my VIP mailing list and get your *free box set* containing three action-packed romances.

Visit here to get started: www.annahackett.com

Would you like a FREE BOX SET of my books?

PREVIEW: HEART OF EON

S he crawled through the tight space, huffing and puffing.

God, she would give anything to be back in her cushy office, or her high-tech, decked-out computer lab. Anything was better than trying to squeeze her curvy ass through a vent tunnel on an alien warship.

An Eon warship that she'd hijacked.

Wren Traynor bumped her elbow against the tunnel

wall and pain shot up her arm. She swallowed a curse and kept crawling. Then her knee scraped on something sharp and she barely swallowed a yelp. That was going to leave a bruise.

The things she did for her sisters.

Suddenly, a clanging sound echoed through the vent tunnel. She stopped, her heart jumping. She knew what that meant. The warriors were searching for her.

And they were getting close.

In the darkness, Wren pulled out her precious tablet and thumbed the screen. It flared to life.

Hmm, time to keep those big, brawny Eon warriors busy doing something else. Plus, get a little bit of enjoyment out of things. She deserved *some* fun since her life had gone to shit.

It had all started five months before, when her older sister, Eve, had been framed for a crime she didn't commit and locked away in a low orbit prison. *Dickwad Space Corps.* Eve had dedicated her life to the Corps, but they'd turned on her in an instant. Then, if that wasn't bad enough, Space Corps had blackmailed Eve into abducting an Eon war commander.

Bad idea. Wren's throat tightened, and she sent up a quick prayer that her sister was okay.

Things had gone from bad to worse when the Corps had approached Wren, offering to free Eve...but only if Wren hijacked an Eon warship, the *Rengard*, using her genius hacker skills.

Oh, and on top of that, the nasty insectoid aliens, the Kantos, were planning to invade and destroy Earth. Yep, her life was complete shit.

Wren sighed. She missed her cushy office and computer lab, she missed her apartment, and she missed her morning lattes. She sighed again. Earth needed the Eon Empire's help, sure, but she was totally unconvinced that abducting them and hijacking their warships was going to convince them to hold hands with Terrans and happily go into battle to save Earth.

Man, her life had definitely gone gurgling down the drain.

You're in over your head, Wren. The voice of her cheating, lying ex-boyfriend echoed in her head.

Smug bastard. She poked her tongue out. No way she was letting that asshole suck up any of her oxygen. She'd kicked his cheating ass out months ago, and even the echo of his voice wasn't welcome.

She tapped on the tablet screen, pulling up the schematics of the ship. Over the last few days, she'd been painstakingly mapping the *Rengard's* layout. Mostly so she could find out-of-the-way washrooms where she could relieve herself, and to keep one step ahead of the warriors.

Suddenly, a deep voice echoed through the tablet's speakers.

"Woman."

She rolled her eyes. War Commander Dann-Jad was a man of few words. Especially when he was angry.

"Good morning, WC," she said.

There was a pause. "WC?"

"War commander is a bit of a mouthful. Although, it's unfortunate that WC is an abbreviation for something *entirely* different on Earth."

There was a charged silence. Wren could practically feel the *Rengard's* war commander reining in his temper.

"Return full control of my ship to me. Now."

Here we go again. She lowered her voice to match his. "You silly Terran woman, return control of my ship to me. I've asked you dozens of times, and every time you've said no, but I'll try again." Wren let her voice return to normal. "Screw you, WC. I've got a planet to save, and a sister to rescue."

And her mission was to get the *Rengard* to a rendezvous point, where they would meet the Space Corps.

She still was uncertain as to how Space Corps thought they were going to subdue Dann-Jad and his fully trained warriors. The Eon warriors, although they shared the same ancestor with the people of Earth, were taller, bigger, stronger, and generally more badass.

Oh, and bonded to a kickass alien symbiont that gave them the ability to create cool armor and weapons with a mere thought.

Of course, during their game of cat and mouse, Dann-Jad had disabled the ship's star drive. That meant they were crawling along at regular, old thruster speed. The journey would take weeks.

And Wren's food supply was dangerously low. She'd run out of chocolate and coffee days ago. Her body was crying out for caffeine. Her rations were down to some freeze-dried disgustingness masquerading as chicken stew and cardboard-flavored nutrition bars. *Blergh.*

Not to mention she smelled bad. She sniffed herself and winced. She'd used her last wet wipe hours ago. She was moving well beyond the desperate need for a shower, and while she risked using the washrooms tucked deep in the bowels of the ship to relieve herself, she didn't dare spend any more time in there. That was all she needed, getting caught with her spacesuit around her ankles by the war commander.

Luckily, I love my sisters. She felt a pang of emotion, hoping, praying Eve and Lara were both okay. Lara had to be so worried.

"Wren Traynor," Dann-Jad growled, "As I told you before, the Eon now have an alliance with Earth—"

"Lies. You're trying to trick me."

"War commanders do not lie or trick." He really sounded pissed now.

"I've got things to do." She stabbed the button on her tablet to stop their little tête-à-tête.

She started crawling again, banged her shoulder, and cursed loudly. She turned a corner, and knew she was close to the *Rengard's* engine room. Scanning the metal wall, she found the maintenance panel she was looking for.

"A-ha." She pulled out her AllDriver and quickly worked the panel off. Then she lifted her tablet, tapping into the *Rengard's* systems. It was a risk, because if the warriors caught her in there, they could pinpoint her location. She tapped on the screen, her fingers flying as she activated the program she'd been working on. She *needed* to get the star drives back online.

She tapped again. *Yes.* Got it.

The vent tunnel vibrated beneath her. She wiggled her booty. "Yes!"

As the engines spooled up, she imagined War Commander Dann-Jad sitting in his cushy office near the bridge, calling her lots of names.

Time to go. She tapped the controls and initiated a jump to light speed that would send them closer to Earth. For a second, it felt like the air around her blurred.

She knew they were now rushing along at the speed of light.

Then suddenly, the ship jolted. Wren's forehead smacked the side of the tunnel. *Jesus.* Rubbing her head, she felt the speed drop away and the vibrations of the engines die.

Damn the man! She screeched and thumped her hand against the wall. Pain radiated up her arm. "Ow."

"You are not hijacking my ship," Dann-Jad's voice came from her tablet again.

He'd hacked her tablet again. Damn, whoever his hacker was, they were good.

"I already have, WC."

She heard his growl. "I'll make you regret your actions."

Too late. She already did.

Wren dragged in a breath. Well, now it was time to keep her war commander busy. So busy, in fact, he wouldn't have time to stop her the next time she got the star drives back online. She swiped her screen, her tongue between her teeth.

There. She grinned and imagined his face. *How do you like that, WC?*

Oh yeah, the small pleasures. It paid to take them when she could find them.

She heard another vicious growl through the tablet, and she could almost imagine him with cartoon steam pouring out his ears.

Now, time to get those star drives working again. Wren started crawling.

WITH A GROWL, War Commander Malax Dann-Jad tugged at the collar of his black uniform. The high-tech fabric was damp with sweat, and perspiration sheened his bare arms.

"Airen!"

His second appeared in the doorway of his office. She was also sweating.

"War commander." Her brown hair was pulled back in a braid, and a few strands were stuck to her damp forehead.

"Status of the ventilation on the bridge level."

"We're still working on it."

Cren. How could one small Terran woman cause all this upheaval?

Malax slammed his fist against his desk. Second Commander Airen Kann-Felis didn't flinch, but the woman's black-green eyes moved to stare at the wall. She'd been his second-in-command long enough to know to ignore his bursts of temper.

"Work harder." The helian symbiont circling Malax's wrist pulsed, reacting to his emotions.

"The Terran has scrambled several systems. The team is doing everything they can." Airen released a breath. "Malax, if we can pump some *daros* gas into the ventilation system—"

"No. She is not to be harmed and I can't risk the gas getting into the rest of the ship."

"It wouldn't kill her."

"Are you an expert on Terran physiology, Airen?"

His second sighed. "No."

"Find another way."

"Yes, sir." Airen pursed her lips, swiveled, and left.

For days, his ship had been under Wren Traynor's control. Lights had been going out, they'd had ventilation problems, and she'd had them jumping all around the Syrann Quadrant before he'd managed to shut down the star drives.

His warriors still couldn't find her, and they'd been searching every maintenance conduit, ventilation tunnel, and storage closet for days.

He pulled in a ragged breath. Malax liked control. Being a war commander was in his blood. He'd been born for the job, like his father before him.

By Alqin's axe, he *would* take back his ship.

He touched the comp screen on his desk, and a picture of Wren Traynor appeared. He stared at her face. She was flanked by her sisters in the image. According to the partial transmissions he'd managed to receive from the *Desteron*, both of Wren's sisters were now, unbelievably, mated to Eon warriors and safe aboard the other warship.

He'd tried sending the transmissions to Wren as proof, but she hadn't let the files through and accused him of trying to implant a bug in her tablet.

His gaze fell on the image again. Wren's sisters were far taller than her. Eve Traynor had managed to abduct the most decorated war commander in the Eon fleet right off his ship. Somehow, after an attack by the Kantos, Eve and Davion Thann-Eon had ended up mated. And then Lara Traynor, after stealing several sacred Eon gems, had ended up mated to the warrior sent to track her down— Davion's security commander, Caze Vann-Jad.

With the Kantos looming, Earth had gotten desperate. One part of Malax understood. The Kantos were ruthless and unforgiving. The bug-like beings swarmed planets, decimating everything in their path. In a risky move, Earth's Space Corps had sent the Traynor sisters to kidnap, steal, and hijack as a way to gain the Eon Empire's attention.

The plan, Malax admitted dryly, had worked.

He looked at Wren's face. She was different from her sisters. The older two were clearly athletic, and both had harder, tougher lines on their faces that said they were used to command and combat. Both were a part of Earth's Space Corps—Eve, a Sub Captain, and Lara, a special forces marine.

Wren was shorter, smaller, and softer looking. It was clear she laughed a lot just from looking at her face.

Malax had grown up with sisters. He had four of them. And after his father had died, Malax had become his family's provider, their protector. So, he knew how to deal with females.

But Wren Traynor was eroding the last of his patience.

His ship was in disarray and at risk. And only his top-level warriors knew, but the *Rengard* had some top-secret, experimental technology buried in the heart of its systems.

Tech he knew their enemies would kill to get their hands on.

Without full control of his ship, any enemy could move in on them. Malax gripped the edge of his desk. It was his responsibility to keep his ship, its tech, and its warriors safe. His gut hardened, old memories bombarding his head. His helian pulsed again.

He pulled in a deep breath. He would *not* lose any of his warriors. Not again.

Once again, he touched his comp, trying to contact her. The warriors on his communications team had done outstanding work to allow him to access her system. Not full access, and not enough to find where she was hiding, but enough to communicate with her.

"Wren Traynor." He stared at the blinking screen, waiting for an answer. "Woman, respond."

"I'm *busy*."

He frowned at the tart response. "Busy destroying my ship."

"God, you're moody."

Malax gritted his teeth so hard he heard a cracking sound in his jaw. "You've hijacked my ship, making it and my warriors vulnerable—"

"I'm too busy to talk right now, WC. Take a chill pill, and we can do some verbal sparring later."

The comm link went dead.

Malax wanted to throw something at the wall. Digging deeper than ever for some control, he sat back in his chair, tugging at his collar. He was angry, hot, and cranky.

And one tiny, Terran woman was to blame.

Eon Warriors

Edge of Eon
Touch of Eon
Heart of Eon
Kiss of Eon
Mark of Eon
Claim of Eon
Storm of Eon
Soul of Eon
King of Eon
Also Available as Audiobooks!

PREVIEW: GLADIATOR

Want more action-packed science fiction romance? Then check out the first book in *Galactic Gladiators*.

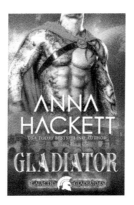

Fighting for love, honor, and freedom on the galaxy's lawless outer rim...

When Earth space marine Harper Adams finds herself abducted by alien slavers off·a space station, her life turns into a battle for survival. Dumped into an arena on a desert planet on the outer rim, she finds herself face to face with a big, tattooed alien gladiator...the champion of the Kor Magna Arena.

A former prince abandoned to the arena as a teen, Raiden Tiago has long ago earned his freedom. Now he rules the arena, but he doesn't fight for the glory, but instead for his own dark purpose--revenge against the Thraxian aliens who destroyed his planet. Then his existence is rocked by one small, fierce female fighter from an unknown planet called Earth.

Harper is determined to find a way home, but when she spots her best friend in the arena--a slave of the evil Thraxian aliens--she'll do anything to save her friend...even join forces with the tough alpha male who sets her body on fire. But as Harper and Raiden step foot onto the blood-soaked sands of the arena, Harper worries that Raiden has his own dangerous agenda...

Galactic Gladiators
Gladiator
Warrior
Hero
Protector
Champion
Barbarian
Beast
Rogue
Guardian
Cyborg
Imperator
Hunter
Also Available as Audiobooks!

ALSO BY ANNA HACKETT

Sentinel Security

Wolf

Hades

Striker

Steel

Excalibur

Hex

Also Available as Audiobooks!

Norcross Security

The Investigator

The Troubleshooter

The Specialist

The Bodyguard

The Hacker

The Powerbroker

The Detective

The Medic

The Protector

Also Available as Audiobooks!

Billionaire Heists

Stealing from Mr. Rich

Blackmailing Mr. Bossman

Hacking Mr. CEO

Also Available as Audiobooks!

Team 52

Mission: Her Protection

Mission: Her Rescue

Mission: Her Security

Mission: Her Defense

Mission: Her Safety

Mission: Her Freedom

Mission: Her Shield

Mission: Her Justice

Also Available as Audiobooks!

Treasure Hunter Security

Undiscovered

Uncharted

Unexplored

Unfathomed

Untraveled

Unmapped

Unidentified

Undetected

Also Available as Audiobooks!

Oronis Knights

Knightmaster

Knighthunter

Galactic Kings

Overlord

Emperor

Captain of the Guard

Conqueror

Also Available as Audiobooks!

Eon Warriors

Edge of Eon

Touch of Eon

Heart of Eon

Kiss of Eon

Mark of Eon

Claim of Eon

Storm of Eon

Soul of Eon

King of Eon

Also Available as Audiobooks!

Galactic Gladiators: House of Rone

Sentinel

Defender

Centurion

Paladin

Guard

Weapons Master

Also Available as Audiobooks!

Galactic Gladiators

Gladiator

Warrior

Hero

Protector

Champion

Barbarian

Beast

Rogue

Guardian

Cyborg

Imperator

Hunter

Also Available as Audiobooks!

Hell Squad

Marcus

Cruz

Gabe

Reed

Roth

Noah

Shaw

Holmes

Niko

Finn

Devlin

Theron

Hemi

Ash

Levi

Manu

Griff

Dom

Survivors

Tane

Also Available as Audiobooks!

The Anomaly Series

Time Thief

Mind Raider

Soul Stealer

Salvation

Anomaly Series Box Set

The Phoenix Adventures

Among Galactic Ruins

At Star's End

In the Devil's Nebula

On a Rogue Planet

Beneath a Trojan Moon

Beyond Galaxy's Edge

On a Cyborg Planet

Return to Dark Earth

On a Barbarian World

Lost in Barbarian Space

Through Uncharted Space

Crashed on an Ice World

Perma Series

Winter Fusion

A Galactic Holiday

Warriors of the Wind

Tempest

Storm & Seduction

Fury & Darkness

Standalone Titles

Savage Dragon

Hunter's Surrender

One Night with the Wolf

For more information visit www.annahackett.com

ABOUT THE AUTHOR

I'm a USA Today bestselling romance author who's passionate about ***fast-paced, emotion-filled*** contemporary romantic suspense and science fiction romance. I love writing about people overcoming unbeatable odds and achieving seemingly impossible goals. I like to believe it's possible for all of us to do the same.

I live in Australia with my own personal hero and two very busy, always-on-the-move sons.

For release dates, behind-the-scenes info, free books, and other fun stuff, sign up for the latest news here:

Website: www.annahackett.com